"Paige!"

She turned on him like a tiger. "No! Don't you dare say one more word to me."

"Paige, please…" His voice held a pleading note.

"No!" she cried once again. Swallowing hard, she turned and gave him a cold and indifferent look.

With hunched shoulders, he met her stare with a grim look in his eyes.

"I want you to promise you won't come here again—ever." The silence that followed these words allowed Paige to continue. "I don't know what kind of game you're playing but…" Again she paused, breathing deeply. "But whatever it is, I don't intend to be a part of it any longer."

"Ms. Baxter sure knows how to hook her readers."

—*Rendezvous*

MARY LYNN BAXTER

TEARS OF YESTERDAY

MIRA

ISBN 1-55166-417-8

TEARS OF YESTERDAY

Copyright © 1982 by Mary Lynn Baxter.

To my husband, Leonard, with love

With special thanks to:
Calvin Evans, owner, The Gold Nugget
Lee Schwartz, owner, Lee's Jewelers
Glenda Pickens, jeweler
and
Charles Dendy, attorney

One

Paige Morgan loved her work and was good at it. She was doing what she loved best and that was designing jewelry of all types, sizes and shapes for all kinds of individuals. There was a challenge to meet every day and when she didn't allow the past to rear its head, she was satisfied with her life.

She was an independent woman, earning a decent living as chief jewelry designer for Wallace Jewelers. Her one burning ambition, however, was to own a small jewelry store specializing in designing and making jewelry.

Now the security of her life and her dream was threatened. She could deal with a marriage that was in trouble; a person learned to work hard and not think about it. But seeing her husband, Lane, was something she abhorred doing. It made the failure of their marriage too real. It reminded her that nothing had changed between them. The separation hadn't fixed things. But she had given her word...

The first order of the day, Paige decided, was to call Lane's office in downtown Houston to make sure he was there or would be later in the day. She didn't intend to say who was calling.

Before losing her nerve, she grabbed the phone and quickly dialed the number she still remembered like her own name. The switchboard operator answered in the usual polite, businesslike tone, "Good morning, Lane Jewelers. May I help you?"

"Yes, good morning," answered Paige, striving to keep her voice calm. "May I please speak to Mr. Morgan?"

"Just one moment and I'll connect you."

While the operator rang the extension, Paige chewed on her lower lip. She recognized Lane's secretary when she finally answered. "Mr. Morgan's office."

Clearing her throat, Paige said, "Could you please tell me if Mr. Morgan will be in his office today?" she crossed her fingers hoping that Mrs. Lindsay didn't recognize her voice. It had been a long time....

"Yes, he's in now. May I say who's calling?"

"No. I'll call back later and make an appointment. Thank you." Her hands shook as she quickly lowered the phone back into its cradle.

Mrs. Lindsay, Paige guessed, probably thought that whoever was on the other end of the phone was some kind of idiot. She certainly felt like one.

Forcing herself to move her shaky legs, she strode to the closet to try and find a suitable outfit. What did one choose to wear to confront an estranged husband of two years to ask him for help? She couldn't believe she was actually going to do it, and hoped it was a dream and she would wake up shortly.

Ignoring the fact that she was postponing the inevitable, she decided to call Sally. Maybe talking to Sally would settle her feelings. She needed to call anyway and let her know there was a possibility she, Paige, wouldn't be at work today.

Sally Patterson, the secretary at the southwest branch of Wallace Jewelers where Paige had her office, was another friend that she couldn't have done without during the past two years. From their first meeting, they had become good friends and confidantes. Sally was the only one who knew any of the true facts about her marriage and separation. But even with Sally, there were still some things that Paige couldn't bear to talk about, even now.

While waiting for Sally to answer, Paige plugged in the set of electric rollers. Her hair needed all the help it could get this morning. It looked like she felt— drained of all energy.

Finally Sally's bright voice sounded over the line, "Hello!"

"My, but you sound in fine form this morning, my friend."

"Oh, hi, Paige," came the chirpy rejoinder. "I do feel good this morning. Wayne came over last night and you know what followed."

"Do I ever," replied Paige, as she laughed. "One of these days you're going to get in trouble playing Wayne and David against each other."

"I hope not, at least not any time soon," Sally said, giggling. "I'm having too much fun."

"Don't say I didn't warn you," Paige teased, already feeling better just bantering back and forth with Sally.

"What's up? Do you want to ride to work with me?"

"No..." Paige hesitated. "I won't be in this morning, nor this afternoon either. I'm hoping to see Lane this morning if I can." She paused to let her words soak in.

Sally gasped! "You're not serious?"

"Oh, I'm serious all right," Paige returned dourly.

"But why? After all this time. I don't understand...?"

Sighing, Paige said, "It's Jamie, Sally. He's run away. Mother was waiting at the door for me yesterday afternoon with the news. He'd left a note to that effect. It's going to take a good lawyer and a lot of money to get him out of trouble." She paused, breathing deeply. "Mother cried and whined until I promised her I'd ask Lane to help us." She was holding the phone so tightly that her arm began to jerk. Just thinking about last night and the bitter words that had passed between her and Katherine made her cringe.

"I hope to hell you know what you're doing, Paige."

"So do I,' she whispered fervently.

"I'm not going to preach to you now," Sally replied. "But if you need me just let me know. And I'm really sorry about Jamie," she added.

Tears gathered in Paige's eyes. "Thanks. I don't

know what I'd do without you to listen to all my trials and tribulations."

"What are friends for?" Sally remarked. "Call me when you can, okay?"

"Okay. I'll talk to you later, then. Bye."

Looking at her watch, Paige noted she had time for a quick cup of coffee, hoping it would help her relax. But that proved not to be the case. As she slowly sipped the hot liquid, her thoughts centered upon her husband.

Still considered young, Lane Morgan was the epitome of success. Everything he touched turned to gold, literally. Lane Jewelers, Inc., his retail jewelry business, was located throughout the United States and abroad. She didn't even know how many stores he had altogether.

He was still active in making sure his stores maintained their high level of quality, according to a recent article in *Jewelers' Magazine*. It quoted Lane as saying: "Our motto at Lane Jewelers is quality before quantity." Judging from his success, his goal had been reached.

The color photograph of a successful Lane Morgan appearing with the article had made him seem threateningly near. His smiling face had jumped off the page at her and had jarred her very soul.

After the thumping of her heart had quieted, she had read the rest of the article. It had gone on to say that once Mr. Morgan had purchased his diamonds in London, they were sent directly to his new cutting factory in Antwerp, Belgium, where they were cut, polished and made into jewelry. Then they were disbursed to all his stores.

The author of the article had compared Lane with the late Harry Winston, who was considered to be the wizard of the diamond business. It was amazing, she thought, how much he had expanded his empire just in the last two years. It seemed as if he were driven by some demon to overpower the entire industry.

Realizing she had wasted more time than she intended, Paige quickly drained the contents of her cup into the sink, and reluctantly made her way to her room to get dressed.

There wasn't much to pick from among the few garments hanging in the closet. She wanted to look her best—for pride's sake if nothing else. But she didn't want Lane to get the wrong idea about the visit either. The only suitable item she had with her was a tailored cranberry ultrasuede skirt and jacket. She had an off-white turtleneck sweater that looked good with it. Her calf-length brown boots completed the outfit.

As she put on her makeup, Paige studied her reflection in the mirror. She wondered if Lane would notice any change in her after two years. Now, at age twenty-five, she was supposed to begin looking for the tiny wrinkles that were to appear after reaching that magic age. According to her unclinical eye, she had none so far. She had a flawless complexion that enhanced the beauty of her dark blue eyes surrounded by thick sooty eyelashes, high cheekbones, and classical straight nose. Her long mahogany brown hair, worn in the latest style—the curly, layered look—formed a natural halo for her fine-boned beauty.

After completing her makeup, she shed the robe and surveyed her naked body in the mirror. She knew she was pretty, with a model's full breasts and shapely legs. Many women were tall and slender. Perhaps it was the overall maturity. The heartbreak and pain she had suffered had given her an indefinable carriage and poise. Would Lane still find her attractive?

By the time she finished dressing, it was nine o'clock. It was now or never, she mused to herself. She had procrastinated long enough.

Paige tried to squelch the sense of panic gnawing at her insides. However, the feeling persisted as she carefully maneuvered her car into the garage that housed the corporate offices of Lane Jewelers, Inc.

After parking successfully, she breathed deeply and briskly walked the short distance to the elevator. Her destination was the top floor of this impressive highrise office building.

She pushed the elevator button, accidentally hit the wrong one and pushed another. By the time she stepped onto the carpeted hallway, twenty-four floors up, her heart was beating so fast that she could hardly breathe. Her stomach, she feared, was certainly going to betray her.

Before anyone could see her in this state, she quickly darted into the nearest ladies' room. Leaning against the door, Paige forced herself to take deep breaths until she managed to get her heaving chest almost back to normal. Now she knew how Daniel must have felt when he walked into the lions' den.

Ignoring the queasy feeling still in her stomach, she squared her shoulders and stepped out to meet the lions.

Upon entering the office, Paige expected to see the ever faithful Mrs. Lindsay at her desk. Instead, she was surprised to see a stranger sitting there. The young girl merely raised her eyebrows in question as Paige walked up to the desk. She willed herself to be calm. ''I'd like to see Mr. Morgan, please.''

Frowning, the secretary asked, ''Do you have an appointment?'' Not giving Paige a chance to answer, she went on to say, ''Mrs. Lindsay had to leave rather suddenly and I'm new at all this.'' Her eyes encompassed everything around her: phone, desk and filing cabinets.

Paige hesitated. She was tempted to lie, but thought better of it. Anyway she needed another breather before she actually confronted Lane. ''No, I don't have an appointment. But if you'll tell him Paige is here, I'm sure he'll see me.''

The secretary looked skeptical but dared not argue. ''Mr. Morgan isn't in his office right now. However, if you'd care to wait…?''

With a resigned sigh, Paige said, ''All right, I'll wait.''

Turning, she made her way to the nearest chair. Surely she wasn't going to faint? Her hands were clammy, and her stomach was rebelling. She simply had to get hold of herself.

She had only been seated a moment and was reaching for a magazine when the door opened rather abruptly. She looked up and locked eyes with her husband.

For several seconds absolute silence deadened the room.

After two years, Lane Morgan hadn't changed one iota. He was even better looking than she remembered. The black hair, now mostly gray, made him look older. But instead of detracting from his looks, it enhanced them. Age thirty-eight definitely agreed with him.

He was as slim as ever. His over six-foot frame showed off his hard-toned muscles that even his designer suit couldn't hide. The only thing different about him was the firm lines etched about his eyes and mouth. They gave his face a grimness that hadn't been there before. His sensual mouth, perfect white teeth and well-define jaw, however, remained the same.

He was too big, too virile and too masculine. Seeing him again reminded her of the past which she simply refused to dwell upon. This encounter made the center of her being throb with desires that she thought were incapable of ever being rekindled. She couldn't afford to let that happen to her—not now—not ever.

Before the silence became embarrassing, he questioned threateningly with darkening eyes. "What are you doing here?"

Paige somehow managed to maintain a cool front. "I came to see you."

Lane shook his head slowly. "Well, I knew if anything would get your attention, it would be the letter. And I see I was right,'' he finished sarcastically.

She flushed. ''I don't know what you're talking about.''

He raised his eyebrows. ''Come on into the office.'' Standing aside, he signaled for her to go ahead of him. Then he turned to the wide-eyed girl and barked, ''Hold all my calls.''

Upon entering his domain, the silence was again so thick that it was overwhelming. Inside, the office furnishings were even more opulent than she remembered.

Without speaking, he indicated she should sit down, nodding to a comfortable chair. Since her legs threatened to crumble, she did as he suggested.

He sat down, too, behind his desk and watched her with guarded scrutiny. She wondered what he was thinking. It wasn't long, however, before she found out. ''Well, Paige, before we get down to business, I must say you're still as beautiful as ever. And talented, too, so I'm told.''

When she made herself look at him, his eyes were resting on her breasts. She felt a quiver of awareness run through her body. Turning away, she said, ''Thank you. You don't look half bad yourself.'' This polite conversation and his staring was making her extremely nervous. She wanted to scream at him!

Sensing her agitation, he said, his eyes more piercing than ever, ''If you didn't come about the letter, then why *did* you come?''

Paige swallowed. ''First of all, I *don't* know what

letter you're referring to. Would it be asking too much for you to tell me?'' she snapped irritably.

Jumping up, Lane glared at her. ''Oh, come off it, Paige. You know very well what letter I'm talking about. Matt sent it to your apartment a week ago.''

''Please, Lane,'' she said as an uneasy feeling overcame her. ''I've been staying with Mother for the past few weeks. I haven't even gone by my apartment to pick up my mail. So for the last time, what was in it?'' Her eyes were full of questions as she followed his roving frame around the room.

Lane's eyes narrowed. ''Can't you guess?'' Seeing the confusion mirrored on her face, his expression became grimmer. ''The *letter* explains the contents of *our* divorce agreement, which requires your signature.''

The only sound in the room was Paige's indrawn breath. After a moment, she shook her head without turning. ''No,'' she mumbled. ''I—I didn't know.''

A chill invaded her bones; when she rose she could hardly feel her legs moving. She stalked to the door. Leaving seems to be the only thing to do, she thought silently. She had to get out of this room before she made a complete fool of herself. The ugly word *divorce, divorce, divorce* kept echoing through her mind. Now, with this added complication, her task seemed impossible.

Her hand was on the doorknob when she inhaled the rich odor of Lane's cologne. It assaulted her senses. Whirling, she found him behind her.

"Paige…" He was looking at her now, his eyes soft and gentle.

"Paige." He repeated again, his voice thick. "If you didn't come about the divorce, then *why* did you come?" He raised his hand as if to reach for her.

Moving away, she hissed, "Don't you dare touch me! Just let me get out of here!"

Lane shook his head adamantly. "I think not. At least, not until you tell me why you're here."

Paige moved to a chair, gripping the back of it. "Forget it," she stated in an emotionless voice. "Why I came is no longer important. I'm sorry, I wasted your time." With those words, she bolted toward the door.

But as she passed her husband, his hand shot out, grabbed her wrist and jerked her around to face him. "You're not going to walk out on me a second time without an explanation," he murmured harshly. "Do I make myself clear?"

Paige flattened herself against the door, despising herself for the havoc his touch had awakened within her. His hard mouth and stubborn jaw were too close for comfort. Not for one moment had she forgotten the delights that his mouth had shown her.

Out of the fog, she heard her voice cry, "Get away from me! You can't stop me from…"

Paige never finished the sentence. There was an urgent knock on the door. The young secretary was trying her best to push her way into the office. However, Paige's limp body sagging against the door was prohibiting her from doing so. Momentarily the secretary managed to peep around the corner.

"Dammit to hell, Vicky, didn't I tell you not to bother me?" bellowed Lane, his face blood red.

"Please, sir," she stammered, "but, but...Mr. Allen is on the phone demanding to talk to you. He said it's urgent and he won't take no for an answer." From the look of sheer terror on Vicky's face, she must have expected her head to roll any minute.

Rubbing the back of his neck in exasperation, Lane finally said in a more controlled voice, "All right, I'll take it." Then he turned to Paige and rasped, "We'll continue this conversation shortly."

The moment he turned his back to walk to his desk to pick up the phone, Paige turned and walked out the door.

From the inner office, she heard him shriek, "Dammit! Paige, wait a minute!"

She wouldn't wait. And she couldn't tell him why she had really come, not now, not after he asked for a divorce. She remained a bundle of nerves until she got out of the building and into her car. Even after locking both doors, she didn't feel safe until she pulled out of the garage into the downtown traffic.

Then she started to cry.

As she drove, Paige struggled to relieve her mind of all thoughts. To think at this point was much too painful. Then, as the tears flowed, so did her thoughts. Why had she let her mother back her into a corner and push her straight into hell? Why had she let her mother talk her into confronting her husband?

As the cars on the freeway passed her, Paige found herself dwelling on her family and their problems...

* * *

After she and Lane had separated, Jamie began going downhill. He began running with the wrong crowd, staying out to all hours, playing hooky from school and drinking. It all culminated, she realized, with the car accident two weeks ago. Her brother and five other boys were drag-racing his car on one of the main thoroughfares and were involved in a wreck in which the elderly occupants of the other car were seriously injured. Jamie was driving. They were all drinking and having a good time and not paying attention to where they were going. Because Jamie was drinking *and* driving, he was the one in the most trouble.

The elderly couple had hired a young attorney who was trying to make a name for himself, and he wanted to make an example out of Jamie. To make matters worse, the insurance on his car had elapsed, so now her mother was personally responsible.

Jamie's running away was the straw that broke the camel's back. Now he was in more trouble than ever. Where would it all end?

The loud honking of a horn jolted Paige out of her reverie. She had veered across the white line down the center of the freeway and barely missed getting hit. Drawing a shaky breath, she forced herself to concentrate for the next few miles on nothing but her driving. She hoped she would get to her mother's house in one piece.

She dreaded what awaited her there.

Two

When Paige finally pulled into the driveway, she was exhausted. In addition, she was shaking like a leaf in a hurricane. How she ever made it this far she didn't know.

Removing her sunglasses, she rested her head on the steering wheel and breathed deeply. She couldn't believe that Lane was actually going to divorce her after two years. This was something she had grown out of the habit of considering.

It was like dying when he had said the word *divorce*. She knew now exactly how it must feel to die. She had felt her life drain of all its will, love and color.

But why was she acting like this? Why was her heart beating so fast? Wasn't that what she wanted—to sever all ties with him? *Yes, of course it is,* she kept telling herself over and over. Then what was the matter with her?

She had to get control of herself and face the truth—her marriage was over and she must start anew. The fact that she wanted to work toward opening her own jewelry store would be her lifeline during the days ahead. But first she must get Jamie's problems straightened out. She groaned aloud—that was another problem in itself, one which had to be faced before she could concentrate on her own future.

Still a little shaky, she got out of the car and made her way into the house. What she needed was two aspirins for her throbbing head. After swallowing these with a little Coke, she went to her room and literally plummeted across the bed.

Perhaps, in a few quiet moments, she could come up with a constructive plan of action for finding her brother and getting the money for a lawyer. There was no way she would or could ask Lane for help now or ever. As it was, she would be a long time healing after this visit. She would have to live daily with the pain it had caused. She and her mother would just have to find another way to get the help they needed.

She was mature, she told herself. She was an educated woman who had known heartbreak. She did *not* intend to grovel to Lane for help!

She fell into a deep and dreamless sleep with this promise on her mind. The next thing she knew, she was rudely awakened by a noise. She glanced at the clock radio beside the bed and noted that it was nearly six o'clock. It must have been the slam of the front door by her mother that jarred her back to consciousness.

She barely had time to collect her thoughts before Katherine walked forcefully into the room, turning on the light. "Well...?" she asked, tension mirrored on her face and in the tone of her voice.

Paige shivered, wrapping her arms around her body. "I'm sorry. I..."

"Oh no!" Katherine cried, after taking a look at her daughter's face. She turned and rested her forehead against the door frame for a moment. "What happened?" she finally asked in a choked voice, raising tear-stained eyes to Paige.

Paige got unsteadily to her feet before answering. "I—I can't talk about it right now. I just can't." She clenched her fist in the hot palm of her hand. "Please don't ask me any questions."

Katherine looked exasperated. "What do you mean you can't talk about it? Don't you care? It must have been your attitude. I know Lane would've helped us. He was so crazy about Jamie."

Paige strove for a patience she didn't feel. She counted to ten before she answered.

"Mother," she said tonelessly, "can't you try to understand? I know it's hard, but there are circumstances that you don't understand and never will. I tried my best to make you see it would be a mistake to approach Lane, but you just wouldn't listen."

"But if you'd..."

Paige jumped up and said, "Please! Let me finish. I'll handle finding Jamie in my own way. Somehow, someway, we'll get a good lawyer and get him out of this mess." She paused to rub the aching muscles in her neck before continuing. "I still think he's hiding out with friends and not in California. I just feel it here." She paused, placing a fist against her stomach.

"Well all right," her mother said petulantly. "I guess I have no choice in the matter."

"That's right," Paige agreed through clenched teeth. "You don't!"

Without another word, her mother turned and walked out of the room. The next sound that reached Paige's ears was the rattle of pots and pans. Katherine was obviously taking her frustrations out on the utensils in the kitchen.

The thought of food almost made Paige turn green. Now that she thought about it, she realized she hadn't eaten anything all day. Maybe that was why her head was still splitting. Since Katherine was going to the trouble to prepare a meal, the least she could do was try and eat a little. But what she really wanted to do was go to bed and nurse her wounds in private.

Wearily, she dragged her tired body to the kitchen a short time later to a meal of warmed-over roast and gravy with green beans and rice. Although the roast tasted like shoe leather, she forced part of it down because she had to eat something.

Throughout the dinner, her mother kept a martyred silence, which was all right with Paige. Anything was better than her mother's wailing and whining.

She finally escaped to the privacy of her room. Before leaving, she had offered to clean up the kitchen, but Katherine shook her head no. Not bothering to argue, Paige went to her room and shut the door.

Leaning against the door, she closed her eyes for a moment and forced herself to relax. Then she began slowly taking off her clothes. A nice hot bath was exactly what she needed to help expel some of the tension.

She longed for the privacy and seclusion of her own apartment. After Jamie had his accident, she had let Katherine talk her into staying with them for a while, hoping she would be a settling influence on her brother. Since Katherine worked three days a week at a day nursery, Jamie was left far too often without close supervision.

While she soaked in the bath, she mapped out a strategy for finding her brother. First thing in the morning, she would make a few more phone calls to her brother's friends—the girls this time—and then call Thomas Forrest, a longtime friend and semiretired attorney, *if* the calls to the girls were not successful. She hated to ask Thomas for help. But unless she came up with another solution, and quickly, she would have no other choice. He had done more than his share for the family. Since Lane was no longer available, her mother called on him often.

After climbing in between the cold sheets, she switched the electric blanket on low and closed her eyes, praying that sleep would come immediately. For a while she tossed and turned. When she finally became still enough, she began to remember the past— the first time she had seen Lane....

She had met him while working in one of his jewelry stores. She had been working part time and attending the University of Houston part time. It had been during an afternoon when two men had come into the store to rob it. Paige had managed to step on the alarm button on the floor and security had arrived in time to keep the thieves from getting away with any jewelry. However, the robbers had noticed what she had done and one of them had opened fire on her and the other employee. A bullet had grazed Paige's temple.

It was at the hospital that she first came into direct contact with Lane. She could vividly remember the first time she saw him. He had walked briskly into the hospital emergency room as if he owned the place.

Even with a severe headache, she was not unaware of the magnetism he radiated. He was the type of man who commanded attention everywhere he went. He drove her to the police station to answer questions as soon as she was released from the hospital. Her wound was minor. The doctor told her a headache would be her only problem. However, he wanted her to take it easy for several days.

For the next three days Lane called to check on her. When the phone rang, her pulse skyrocketed. Their conversations were leisurely, about things that meant nothing. Paige revelled in the sound of his deep voice and couldn't remember half the things he said.

What kind of game was he playing? she wondered as they talked. Why was he calling? Please don't hurt me, she prayed every time she picked up the receiver and heard his voice.

Finally, the day before she was due to return to work, Lane said, "Will you have dinner with me?"

"With *you?*" she returned in disbelief.

He laughed. "Yes. Tomorrow night."

"Why, I—"

"Good. I'll pick you up at seven."

The restaurant was small and elegant. Lane guided her into the entrance and, as they waited to be seated, neither spoke. As if they were isolated from the world, they stood gazing at each other.

"Mr. Morgan?" said the head waiter, hesitantly stepping to Lane's side. Paige returned the smile curving Lane's mouth and took a small breath as he deliberately stepped nearer.

The waiter gently cleared his throat. "Mr. Morgan, this way, please."

They were ushered to a secluded corner which afforded them complete privacy. After ordering their predinner drinks, Paige's eyes roamed around the room. Her hands clutched tightly in her lap to quell their shaking. She still could not believe that she was sitting here having dinner with this man.

She turned without warning and caught Lane's gaze, warm and intent, upon her. She wet her dry lips and let out her breath, not realizing she had been holding it.

"Now that you have looked the place over, could I have your attention?" he questioned huskily.

Her fingers flew to her lips at the expression in his eyes. Slow down, she warned herself. This man could be dangerous. Men of his wealth and prestige did not get seriously involved with mere part-time help.

"I'm sorry. I—" She linked and unlinked her fingers. Then she forced a sparkling smile. "What do you want to talk about?"

Lane's lips twitched knowingly. "For starters, you can tell me about yourself," he said.

Oh, damn, she thought. He was positively enjoying her naiveté. She leaned forward and said, quite seriously, "There's not much to tell, Mr. Morgan."

"Let me be the judge of that," he remarked indolently.

He coaxed it out of her, piece by piece—her dreams of owning her own jewelry shop one day. When the waiter interrupted with their dinner, she expelled a sigh of relief. She hated talking about herself.

They had both refused the salad bar, so when the waiter placed her filet mignon and baked potato in front of her, she hoped she would be able to eat all of it. However, she doubted it—not with the way her stomach was tied in knots.

Throughout the meal, Lane put her at ease with stories about his trips abroad and amusing anecdotes associated with the jewelry business.

She felt herself relax. Her eyelids started to droop. As the waiter quietly removed their dessert dishes and served them coffee, she braced her chin on a fist.

Lane took a long draw from his pipe and leaned back in his chair. "I want you to continue telling me about yourself. Go on," he urged. "Tell me about Paige McAdams."

"Please, Mr. Morgan, I..."

"My name is Lane," he said, measuring his words, his eyes not releasing hers.

Paige nibbled nervously at her lower lip. "All right,

Lane. But I'd really rather not talk about myself anymore. By the way what time do you have?''

Lane glanced at his watch. "It's about ten-fifteen. Why? Are you taking medicine?''

Paige was astounded by his remark. Where had the time gone?

"It's still early," he remarked, his voice low and caressing. "You don't have to go yet.''

To her surprise, he reached across the table and touched her hand. One by one, he curved her fingers over his until their hands were entwined. He smiled.

Paige felt herself burning.

"Please..." she said and paused, willing herself to remain calm, before continuing. "I need to go. I have a seven o'clock class in the morning.''

"Oh?" He obviously didn't believe her.

"Plus tomorrow is my late night to work!" she added hastily. "And—" she broke off. What was wrong with her? She was acting like an idiot.

His thumb gently seduced the inside of her palm.

"Why are you on edge?" he questioned softly. "And scared?''

Her look pleaded with him. "Please, Mr. Morgan," she protested softly, trying to draw her hand from his.

"Lane?''

"All right, then. Lane," she added breathlessly.

"Don't be afraid of me. I'm not going to hurt you.'' His eyes lowered, traveling slowly across the fresh young loveliness of her face down to the burgeoning fullness of her breasts.

When he looked at her like that, the air crackled

with electricity. It was too late and she knew it. She could never be indifferent to this man, no matter how hard she tried.

She turned away, not knowing what to say. For several moments, he did nothing. Then he chuckled at her shyness. "Okay, you win. I'll take you home."

As he was helping her with the chair, he whispered in her ear from behind. "Anyway, I can't have you fall asleep on me now, can I? It would be bad for my image," he finished with a grin.

The drive back to her house was short. She regretted that the evening was over. She had enjoyed herself more than she cared to admit. The bottom line was that she was afraid she wouldn't see him again. Although he had been most attentive these past few days and especially tonight, she was positive she was just a passing fancy to him.

Sure enough, after seeing her safely to the door, he smiled and told her to be sweet and to take care. He then left her without so much as a glance backward.

It was almost a week before she heard from him again. But from then on, they began seeing each other almost every night and sometimes during the day as well. They dined, danced and flew to New York City to see two Broadway shows.

When they were alone, they spent much of their time talking about jewelry. Paige loved the world of precious stones and never got tired of asking Lane about the designing end of the business. She had started a small portfolio of settings for rings and necklaces. One evening Lane forced her to show it to him, and to her surprise, he was quite complimentary.

After that, he took her on several buying trips to New York's Forty-seventh Street, the greatest diamond market in the world. She loved every minute they spent there.

They attended parties together. And fresh flowers arrived daily. Her family thought he was great, especially Jamie. Lane always made an effort to spend time with him, even if it was only a few minutes.

Paige was completely over the awkwardness of their first dinner date and really began to delight in his attention. There was no doubt in her mind—she was *definitely* in love. At age twenty she had succumbed to the charms of a man thirteen years older than herself.

At times Lane indulged her to the point of treating her like a child. But at other times, the burning desire in his eyes made her flesh burn. She wanted his touch. Although he kissed her often, he kept his emotions under control. She was beginning to think maybe something was wrong with her and that maybe she didn't attract him in that way. Then she would remember the passion she had seen in his eyes.

Why was he holding back? These questions preyed on her mind. She thought of various answers but the only one that made any sense was that he didn't feel the same about her as she felt about him.

This feeling was more or less confirmed when he went to Europe suddenly and left her for two weeks. The days dragged by, each one seeming longer than the other. He called her several times, but it wasn't the same. She worked and went to school, but she felt only half alive.

The last time he phoned he made arrangements for her to meet him at the airport. Paige was so excited she could hardly contain herself. When the time came for the plane to land, she waited with eager anticipation.

As soon as Lane's lithe frame emerged through the concourse doors, she hurriedly made her way toward him. She stood in front of him, her lips parted in eager anticipation.

"Hi," he said, smiling. His eyes traced the curve of her lovely face, but instead of claiming the lips so freely offered, he reached over and folded her into his arms for a quick hug.

Paige was puzzled. He seemed aloof.

Pulling slightly away from him, she asked hesitantly, "How was your trip?"

"Great, just great," he answered as he clasped her hand in his and began walking down the concourse.

"I'm glad." Her voice held a tremor.

"How have you been?"

"Oh, fine…just fine."

Paige glanced at him out of the corner of her eye, realizing they were playing out an empty charade.

Silence remained between them until she couldn't stand it any longer.

"Lane, what's wrong?"

He hesitated for an instant. "Nothing," he said but without conviction in his voice.

Her heart plunged. Was he sorry he had asked her to meet him? At times this man was an enigma to her unsophisticated mind.

Most of the other passengers had already departed; the parking lot was almost deserted.

"I have my car," she said, and gestured with a turn of her hand.

But the only comment he made was, "I'll drive."

He unlocked the door on the passenger side and helped her into the car. His large frame was completely out of place in her small Chevette. She wanted to tease him about it and try and relieve some of the tension, but thought better of it. A scowl was plastered on his face.

Sighing, she leaned against the headrest and fought back tears. This homecoming was not what she had expected. She had been looking forward to being in his arms again. Two weeks away from him had been sheer misery. She felt his gaze scan her face from time to time, but he never divulged what was uppermost in his mind.

Without warning, Lane turned toward her and said, "We're having dinner at my apartment this evening. Is that all right with you?"

Because of the lump in her throat, all she could do was shake her head affirmatively. At least he's not going to leave me at home, she told herself.

Lane had never taken her to his apartment. In fact, when she thought about it, she didn't know much about him, except that his parents were dead and that he had a married sister with two children living in

Dallas. He talked about them often but had never taken her to meet them.

The silence in the car was beginning to wear on her nerves when they pulled into the underground garage of his apartment building. His apartment in downtown Houston covered the top floor of the high-rise. As they rode the elevator, the tension was apparent in both of them.

She tried not to look at him, but her eyes kept straying back to his face, tracing the hard lines and the thickness of his hair. He looked strained, white shadowy lines prominent around his mouth.

After making their way down the carpeted hallway, Lane dug into his pocket for his key, unlocked the door and stepped aside for her to enter. A manservant walked around the corner at the same time and, smiling, greeted them both.

''Paige, this is Joseph.''

She returned his smile with great effort.

Leaving the small entry hall, Paige felt the plush carpet beneath her feet as she stepped down into the sunken den. The room was beautiful, and she stood for a moment in awe as she took in the surroundings. The ceiling was high, supported by cedar beams. Mint green carpet grazed the floor, complementing the cream-colored draperies, pulled back to show the wide expanse of glass which covered one whole wall of the room. A large fireplace surrounded by bookcases and a stereo system dominated the other end. Contemporary pine furniture, paintings and plants further enhanced the room.

Lane stood behind her, amused that she was so enthralled with everything. "I'm pleased that you like what you see," he remarked dryly.

She spun around to face him. "Oh, I love it. It's like a room out of a magazine!" she exclaimed, her eyes sparkling. "Am I really here?"

"Yes," he smiled. "You are. Would you care for a glass of Chablis before dinner?"

Paige ran her tongue over her lips. "Yes," she said hesitantly, "but only a thimbleful, please. You know I can't..."

Lane swore softly. "Don't start that business about you can't do this or that. I'm not in the mood to hear it. One drink *won't* hurt you."

She turned away, but not before he saw the hurt that sprang into her eyes.

"God, I'm sorry," he muttered, scraping a hand over his roughened chin.

Paige remained silent, unable to say it was all right, or that she understood.

He crossed to the bar and poured her some wine and mixed himself a Martini, before dropping wearily into the nearest chair. Joseph had built a small fire. Although it was only early October, a light norther had blown in the day before, and after the sun went down, it had become quite chilly. Right now, though, Paige felt her nerves had more to do with her being cold than the weather itself.

If his humor didn't improve shortly, she was going to demand he take her home. But what she really wanted to do was throw her arms around him and beg him to tell her what was the matter, only her pride wouldn't let her do that.

Was this the real Lane Morgan she was seeing today? Had she been deceived all this time? Her thoughts were driving her crazy.

Breaking into her troubled doubts, Lane said, "Would you like to see the rest of the apartment and then freshen up before dinner?"

With a resigned sigh, she stood. "Very well."

The rest of the apartment consisted of two bedrooms with adjoining baths, a kitchen-dining room combination and a large study. All the rooms were done in the same luxurious taste as the den.

The dominating force in Lane's room was the huge king-size bed. Paige's eyes were glued to it. She felt her face flush at her boldness, but she couldn't move or say anything.

Lane brusquely interrupted her thoughts. "Come on. Joseph will be serving dinner shortly."

He actually had to propel her out of the room. Fantasies of Lane and her entwined together on that bed were dancing before her eyes. She was positive that he read her mind—his jaw tightened and an odd look sprang into his eyes.

The impossibility of her dreams sent a tremor passing through her body.

During dinner, Lane was broodingly silent. She couldn't read the expression mirrored in his eyes. He was an expert at hiding his thoughts.

After Joseph removed the dishes, Paige's stomach immediately began to feel really queasy. She hadn't eaten very much but beads of perspiration popped out on her forehead and her hands felt clammy. She barely made it to the bathroom before she lost the contents of her stomach. Lane had followed her.

Moaning, she tried to push him away, but he wasn't to be deterred. He was determined to help her. He put a cold washcloth to her forehead and one to the back of her neck, half carrying her back into the den.

"Oh, God, are you all right?" Her face was still void of color and he was frightened.

"I'm fine," she said weakly. Taking the washcloth out of his hand, she wiped her eyes and mouth and continued in a stronger voice. "Actually I feel better than I have all evening. The food was just too rich," she finished lamely.

She felt like a fool! She was so embarrassed that she couldn't even look him in the eye.

"Honey?" he questioned softly.

Paige trembled, refusing to look up.

He grasped her chin and forced her to look at him. "Would you like to take a shower while Joseph washes your clothes? You're a mess," he finished with a teasing grin on his face. His hands were busy pushing her hair back from her face with maddening deliberation.

"Could I really?" she asked eagerly.

"You betcha," he said, pulling her gently to her feet.

The hot shower beating down on her body felt delicious. She revelled in it. Now that she had gotten sick, Lane seemed more like his old self. How long would it last? She still didn't know what had caused his ill humor in the first place.

Pushing these thoughts aside, she stepped out of the shower and slowly dried herself, postponing the time when she would have to rejoin Lane. She wouldn't be able to take it if he was rude to her again.

She donned a silk robe she found hanging on the back of the door. It was obviously Lane's since it reeked of his manly smell. After brushing her hair and teeth, she walked barefoot into the den.

The indirect lighting had been softened and the fire was creating images on the wall. The room was cozy and she became heady with excitement and anticipation at the warm look radiating from Lane's eyes. He was standing in front of the fireplace with a drink in his hand. He had removed his coat and tie and unbuttoned his shirt.

His eyes glittered over her soft curves with a gaze that raised her blood pressure.

Setting his glass down, he said huskily, "Come here."

Paige didn't hesitate. She glided toward him with her heart in her eyes.

A flicker of uncontrolled emotion burned beneath his jutting brows. "When you look at me like that, you're asking for trouble," he said in a husky voice. His hands reached out and tightened like steel clamps around her rib cage, drawing her into his arms.

Paige nestled close and breathed a sigh of contentment. This was where she longed to be.

Lane rocked her in his arms for a moment. The only

sound in the room was the pulsating beat of their hearts. He finally whispered in her ear, his voice strangled. "I hurt, Honey."

She drew him deeper into the warmth of her soft body, her nipples hardening at the closer contact. "Why?" she questioned gently.

"I hurt so badly," he muttered again as if she hadn't spoken. "My insides are torn to pieces from wanting you. I go to bed wanting you, I wake up wanting you, and like some love-starved teenager, I want you all the damn day, too!"

Paige moistened her dry lips. "I want you, too," she whispered. Barely pausing, she went on softly. "Why don't you quit talking and kiss me?" She couldn't believe she was actually begging Lane to make love to her.

Groaning, he pushed her away abruptly. Raking his hands through his hair, he said, "I can't take much more of this without making you mine."

"I don't know what you want me to say." She was confused and uncertain and totally unsure of what he expected of her. Was he upset with her innocence? Was he afraid she wanted a commitment from him?

His expression hardened. "Dammit, I'll tell you what I want you to say," he groaned out harshly. "I *want* you to tell me that I'm too old for you and that we have no future together. I didn't intend for things to go this far...oh, hell!" he continued, and began pacing around the room like a caged panther. "Who am I trying to kid..."

Paige winced. "Why are you doing this to us?" she

cried. "What's wrong?" She had known this moment was coming.

He closed his eyes for a moment, his long lashes brushing gently against his cheeks. "You just don't understand," he said bleakly, flexing his tight muscles.

"Don't you want me?" Her whispered question fell into the silence like raindrops on a tin roof.

Turning swiftly, he gave her a look so filled with desire that it scorched her skin. "You really and truly have no idea what it does to a man to feast his eyes upon a sweet young body like yours and know that he shouldn't take advantage of what is offered."

Touch me! Kiss me! she screamed at him silently.

Out loud, she whispered, "Lane...I..."

He had reached the breaking point. He moved suddenly and the next thing she knew she was immersed once again within the circle of his arms and his mouth was crushing hers.

It was an all-consuming experience as his lips devoured hers. She felt dizzy from the impact. Boldly she unbuttoned his shirt and tangled her hand in the matted hairs on his chest, trying to maintain a hold on reality.

Her touch only inflamed him more. His tongue entwined with hers, drawing the sweet nectar from her mouth, making it part of his own. His hands fondled her breasts and moved down over her hips and thighs in intimate exploration.

"Paige..."

The passionate use of her name against her mouth

rendered her incapable of being anything except putty in his hands—to mold as he pleased.

Although she had no experience in knowing how to please a man, her need for him was so great that it overcame any inhibition she might have. She wanted to respond to him and her moan was a plea for possession.

With unhurried movements, he untied the silk sash around her waist and devoured her with his eyes as the robe fell to the floor, leaving only the firelight to show off the exquisite beauty of her naked body.

Realizing that she was standing before his piercing eyes unclothed, Paige tried to cover herself with her hands.

"No!" he gasped, as he reached out to cup the swollen fullness of her breasts. He touched first one then the other before replacing his fingers with his mouth, drawing on her nipples until she cried out.

"Oh, please don't stop me," he muttered incoherently. "But if I take you now, I'll never let you go."

Paige was bemused. She had never been this close to a man nor ever thought about allowing the liberties that were taking place. But she didn't want him to stop.

The next thing she knew, she was being lifted in his arms. He laid her gently down on the king-size bed and never took his eyes off her while he peeled his shirt from his body, leaving his lean frame bare to the waist. Then his hand reached for his belt buckle...

From the soft glow of the night light, the sight of

his nakedness completely removed what little sanity she had left. Her limbs trembled with desire.

As he lay beside her, they fused together, flesh against flesh. His hands sought and found the sweet secret delights of her body. His kisses were long, drugging kisses, building a need inside her.

"Please don't be afraid," he moaned as his body covered hers. His lips parted her trembling mouth. "I promise not to..." Instinctively she arched her body to meet the driving force of his and no further words were necessary. Her arms refused to let him go. They basked as one in the fulfillment they had created.

Nothing could have been more beautiful....

Lane had awakened her about one o'clock that morning wanting to talk. She was perfectly content to lie beside him in the warm bed and have his hands caress her forever, but that was not to be.

"Paige..." he had said, "I don't intend to let you go, ever. I want to hear you purr like a kitten, all soft and warm, cuddled up to my backside every morning for the rest of my life. How do you feel about that?"

"Anything you say," she said, stretching languorously.

The movement caused the cover to slip and one rose-tipped breast exposed itself to Lane's eyes. Before she could snuggle back under the covers, his lips had fastened on it. Sensations of pure delight rippled through her body and their love play started all over again.

Their wedding took place one week later.

* * *

They were married for two years and the first one was idyllic. But it bothered her that Lane refused to let her work or go to school. He wanted her to stay home. However, he was gone so much on business that she became bored with the country club life and doing what she termed "unnecessary nothings." When Lane was home, they always seemed to be entertaining or attending someone else's party.

To while away the lonely hours, Paige experimented with designing jewelry. She added different mountings to her portfolio, plus descriptions of the gems she thought should be put into them. Precious stones of all types, but especially diamonds, fascinated her. Many times, when Lane was gone, she would go to the jewelry store where she worked before they married and watch the in-house designer make wax molds for rings and necklaces. She also spent hours watching him melt the gold and then pour it into molds.

Paige begged Lane to let her work and try her hand at designing at one of his stores, but he rejected the idea, suggesting that if she was bored, they should have a baby. They argued often, with him accusing her of only marrying him to further her own career.

For the next year, their relationship deteriorated, and it wasn't long before Lane moved out of their bedroom and they more or less became strangers living under the same roof. When she couldn't take the hostility any longer, Paige moved out of the apartment while he was gone on one of his many trips abroad. Her mother had insisted that she live with her and Jamie until she found a job and an apartment.

Paige was miserable. If it hadn't been for her mother, she would have gone home before Lane returned from his trip. But Katherine kept insisting she wait and let him find her gone and then maybe he would loosen up and let her do some of the things she wanted to do. Paige was positive that when he got home and found her gone, he would come looking for her.

Paige missed him terribly and began to suspect that she was going to have Lane's baby.

A month passed and there was still no word from Lane. She became increasingly distraught. Her pregnancy had been confirmed and she wanted to share the news with him, hoping to bridge the gap between them. Why hadn't he contacted her? She asked herself this question a hundred times. She was positive he was back home. She knew he was furious with her, but surely, she thought, he would make some effort to get in touch with her.

The next day Paige *did* receive word from her husband but not in the way she expected. She remembered walking down the driveway to the mailbox in the cold mist of the day. The first item she saw there was a letter from Lane's attorney.

With a premonition of doom, she ripped open the envelope as she walked back toward the house. Inside was a curt note from Lane stating that the attached papers needed her signature in order to make their separation legal. It went on to say that any further communication between them would be through their lawyers. It was a cold, degrading letter.

By the time she reached the front steps, she was crying so hard she couldn't see where she was going. What happened next was a blur in her mind. Paige felt her foot slip out from under her and then, all she could remember was complete blackness.

When she came to, she was in the hospital and found out she had been there for several days. Her first thoughts were of the baby, and her worst fears were realized. She had lost the one thing that would have brought Lane back to her and bound him to her forever—their baby. Along with the miscarriage, she had received a concussion and developed pneumonia as a result of her exposure to the weather.

Paige was bitter, resentful and sick. She blamed Lane. She was convinced that he had never loved her or he would have come to her when she had needed him.

After the pain and disillusionment subsided, she was able to block thoughts of her husband completely out of her mind. Occasionally, however, she would pick up a newspaper and find Lane's picture staring back at her and her heart would race for a moment. There was a lot of speculation and gossip about their relationship which she belligerently chose to ignore.

She couldn't understand why he never filed for a divorce. But knowing Lane, she was certain he had a reason. Sooner or later she knew there would be a confrontation. Because she was busy and happy with her work, she was able to keep that troublesome thought at bay.

From that time on, her life had more or less settled into a routine. Until now.

Three

When the alarm clock sounded in her ear at six o'clock, Paige was tempted to roll over, turn it off and forget about it. She was exhausted and depressed. Her night of memories left her longing for something she had hoped was dead.

After a quick shower, she gulped down a cup of coffee, then proceeded to make more phone calls which she trusted would produce her brother. As before, she came up empty-handed. She breathed deeply, trying to quell the sense of helplessness that surrounded her.

While she dressed, her thoughts returned once again to Lane and their forthcoming divorce. Soon, she would be free. She kept telling herself she was glad that phase of her life was over, but somehow the gladness never quite reached her heart.

Paige was pale and heavy-eyed when she entered the rear door of her office in the Galleria shopping complex. Ron Wallace was late in arriving, she noticed, and expelled a sigh of relief. Now she would have a little extra time to get herself together.

The only sound in the quiet building was the muffled pounding of Sally's typewriter in the office adjacent to hers. Shedding her coat and depositing her purse in the file cabinet, Paige reluctantly headed toward her friend's office. Since she hadn't called Sally last evening, her friend would be on pins and needles to hear what had transpired between Lane and herself. Paige hated the thought of reliving that scene with Lane but Sally wouldn't give her a moment's peace until she had told her all the gory details.

Tapping lightly on the door, Paige plastered a smile on her face and said, "Good morning."

"Oh, hi, Paige. I didn't hear you come in."

"I guess not. You were hard and fast at work. That new typewriter you have is the noisiest thing I've ever heard."

Sally laughed. "I know, but it types like a dream. You ought to try it sometime."

Paige rolled her eyes. "I think not. You wouldn't want me to usurp your position, now, would you?" she finished in a teasing manner.

Sally merely smiled and looked at Paige intently. "You've stalled long enough, my friend. Let's have it. I finally gave up hearing from you last night and went to bed. Why didn't you call?"

Paige swallowed. "I just couldn't. By the time I got to mother's yesterday afternoon, I was so upset I didn't even know my name." Tears began to fill her eyes at the mention of yesterday. "And, of course, there was the devil to pay when mother got home."

Sally sighed. "I take it things didn't go well with you and Lane?"

"That's an understatement. It was hell, pure and

simple. But, thank God, I don't ever have to see or talk to him again.''

Sally looked puzzled. "I don't follow you. You might as well give me a blow-by-blow account. It might help you to talk about it.''

"All right,'' Paige sighed, brushing the tears off her cheeks. "But first I need a caffeine fix. Is the coffee made?''

"Yes,'' Sally answered. "I felt rotten myself this morning, so I've already had two cups,'' she said, laughing. "But it didn't help much. I still feel hung over.''

"Well, you look like a million bucks to me. But then you always do.'' Paige eyed her friend closely. But it was more than good looks that endeared Sally to her. She was a nice and kind person, easy to talk to and fun to be with. Her short curly blond hair, blue eyes and shapely body drew attention wherever she went. Paige valued her friendship highly.

As she set her coffee mug onto a table in the employee's lounge, Paige glanced at her watch; it was only thirty minutes until opening time. They wouldn't have long to visit.

"Sally, since we don't have much time and Ron's due any minute, can't we postpone this chat until lunch?'' She sighed. "I'm not sure I'm up to baring my soul right now. I have to face Mrs. Frazier this morning.''

This last statement drew a chuckle from Sally. "I know exactly what you mean about Mrs. Frazier, but you might as well tell me a little of what happened yesterday. You can leave the worst 'til later if you want.''

"All right," Paige sighed. "As you already know, Jamie's run away. 'Split the scene' was his way of putting it.'' She laughed bitterly. "Anyway, to make a long story short, we think he caught a ride, hoping to get to California."

"What!" Sally exclaimed, frowning. "Do you mean…''

"Yes, that's exactly what I mean. He's nowhere to be found around here. I've exhausted his source of friends, both male and female. So I can only assume that he's left Houston.'' She pinched the bridge of her nose. "*And* you can imagine how my mother took all of this."

Sally shook her head. "Knowing how Katherine dotes on that boy, I can imagine her reaction." She hesitated. "But she had no right to talk you into going to see Lane."

Paige merely shrugged. She tried to swallow the lump lodged in her throat.

"Well, is he going to help you?" Sally asked softly.

Paige felt her stomach turn over. "No…" She bit her lower lip to keep it from trembling. "Actually, I never, er…I never told him why I went to see him."

Sally tilted her head in puzzlement. "I'm afraid I don't follow you. You don't mean to say that you went to see Lane, after all this time, and didn't even tell him why!" She looked at Paige as if she had taken leave of her senses. "Surely I misunderstood you?"

"No," whispered Paige, barely loud enough for

Sally to hear. Her throat tightened. "Oh, Sally," she finally cried, "he wants a divorce!"

"Oh, my God, oh, my God," repeated Sally in a horrified voice. "But...but why after all this time? I just don't understand."

"Neither do I," returned Paige bitterly. "But as usual, when I need him he never comes through."

"Paige, I'm sorry." Sally leaned forward sympathetically. "I really opened a can of worms by making you rehash all this again, didn't I?" She struck her temple with the heel of her hand. "I should have kept my mouth shut. Will you forgive me?"

All Paige could do was nod affirmatively. She felt like she was choking to death. Why did she react this way every time she mentioned the word *divorce?* She should be glad that Lane would no longer retain any hold on her. She had her career and her dream.

Paige finally forced herself to breathe deeply and assume an outward calm. The thought of breaking down completely, even in front of Sally, was humiliating.

Trying desperately to dispel the mood she had created, Sally said in a upbeat tone, "Well, you don't need Lane anyway. I'm sure Ron will..."

"No!" Paige interrupted. "Please don't mention one word of this conversation to him. He seems to have enough on his mind lately without adding my problems to his load."

Sally frowned. "Well, if you don't ask Ron for help, how do you plan to find Jamie before the authorities do?"

Paige tightened her lips. "I don't know yet. But I will. I don't have a choice. There's always Thomas. I hate to ask him for any further help, but I will if I have to."

"Well," Sally said, "I want to apologize again for raking you over the coals. When you're ready to talk, just remember I'll be available. If there is anything I can do toward finding Jamie, you had better let me know."

"Thanks," Paige replied in a husky voice as she squeezed Sally's hand. "You can rest assured that I'll take you up on that offer." She sighed. "I'll have a few difficult months ahead of me."

"What about lunch today?" Sally asked on a brighter tone and changing the subject.

Paige lifted her brows. "I doubt I'll be able to make it. Mrs. Frazier wants me to design her a set of pierced earrings, a necklace and a ring to match. It'll take all morning, and probably part of the afternoon." She hunched her shoulders. "And you know what a pain she can be."

Sally laughed knowingly as she gathered their cups and rinsed them out in the sink. "I guess I'd better get back to my desk before the boss arrives. He left me a lot of typing to do, and I haven't made a dent in it."

"You go ahead. I need to repair my makeup a little before I encounter Mrs. Frazier."

"Okay," Sally said, smiling. "But let me know about lunch."

After Sally left, Paige stepped into the ladies' room.

She touched up her makeup and ran a comb through her thick hair. She still looked washed out, but presentable enough.

She had just sat down at her desk and retrieved her scratch pad and pencil when she heard Ron come in the back door. When he appeared, she greeted him with an absent smile. Ron, however, was astute enough to quickly notice the pallor of her skin and the tired lines imprinted around her eyes. His thoughtful appraisal deepened to concern when she lifted her face to meet his steady gaze.

"Are you ill or just tired?" he inquired as he parked himself in front of her desk. Ron was a large man in his late twenties whose presence couldn't be ignored. He was of medium to stocky build with an angular face and body. He wasn't handsome, but his gentle brown eyes and easygoing manner took him a long way. And he was aiming for the top.

He was ambitious. He envied Lane Jewelers' success and seemed determined to try and rise to the same plateau. But to her way of thinking, it was an impossible task.

Paige didn't deceive herself; Ron would like their relationship to be more than that of employee and employer. Knowing she was married, although unhappily, he never overstepped the bounds of being just a good friend. But, she had seen the look in his eyes when he thought she wasn't looking. He never mentioned Lane, nor did she.

His attitude was persistent. "What happened yesterday? Why didn't you come to work? You should take my advice to heart and quit burning the candle at both ends.''

Paige summoned a faint smile. ''Please, Ron, don't talk down to me. I know you mean well, but I have no choice. I have to help mother get through this mess with Jamie.''

He studied her impatiently. ''I've told you over and over I'll do anything I can to help you. But you just won't ask me.'' He shrugged his shoulders wearily. ''And I'd like to know why?''

Paige heaved a weary sigh. ''Ron, it's not that I don't want your help.'' She spread her hands. ''It's just that I know you have more than you can handle right now. I simply refuse to add to your burden.''

''You let me be the judge of what I can handle.'' He eyed her intently. ''I'll never be too busy to help you,'' he continued in a softened tone.

Paige keenly sensed the veiled meaning behind his mildly spoken words. She squirmed in agitation. ''Ron, please, let's not discuss it anymore right now, okay? Mrs. Frazier is due any minute.'' She pointedly began scratching on the pad in front of her.

Ron hesitated a moment longer and then with a soft expletive made his way into his office, firmly closing the door behind him. Paige breathed a sigh of relief. She didn't mind telling him about Jamie's latest stunt, but she dreaded him finding out about her encounter with Lane.

She was positive he would insist on pitching in and helping her and for a reason she was loath to admit, even to herself. She didn't want to be obligated to him.

She had seen that certain look in his eyes too many
times. Further complications in this matter were not
for her. At this time, she doubted her ability to enjoy
a full relationship with any man again. She was
tempted to bluntly tell Ron he was wasting his time.

Recently, there had been a difference in Ron's attitude. She couldn't pinpoint the difference, but it was
there nevertheless. She and Sally had discussed it
many times without producing a reason. He seemed
preoccupied and worried. Paige was afraid he might
have bitten off more than he could chew when he had
opened the new store in New York City.

During the rest of the morning Paige was occupied
with Mrs. Frazier. As soon as she arrived, Paige ushered her into the comfortable lounge area located to
the right of the main salon. There were plush chairs
and a glass-topped table where the client viewed the
designs.

Mrs. Frazier brought with her several diamonds of
different sizes along with several other gems, which
she wanted Paige to use, if possible. Paige concen-
trated first on the ring. She had to design something
that would give graceful lines to her client's long fingers. After discarding many rough drafts of various
designs, she finally came up with one that Mrs. Frazier
was enthusiastic about. The ring was sketched in the
shape of a honeysuckle flower. The main branch
would be cast in yellow gold and mounted on platinum. The real touch of class would come when the
petals were added in baguette diamonds of canary yellow. The stems of the honeysuckle were to be made

of emeralds cut into baguettes. The pierced-ear studs and necklace would match.

When this transaction was completed, Mrs. Frazier smiled. "Now, Paige," she paused to settle her large frame more comfortably in the chair, "there's one more special 'something' I want you to do for me." Her smile grew wider. "I want you to make me a pair of gold studs and pendant in the shape of cockroaches."

"What!" Paige exclaimed with a laugh. She didn't even try to mask her astonishment.

Mrs. Frazier sat up straighter in the chair. "You heard me, Paige, dear. For some reason, those little creatures have always fascinated me. Do you think you can handle my request?"

Paige, reached for a sharp pencil. "Oh, yes, ma'am," she returned, "I'll not only handle it, I'll design you the fanciest pair of roaches seen anywhere in Southeast Texas!"

"That sounds just fine," Mrs. Frazier exclaimed, bubbling. "Call me as soon as you get the molds ready."

"Oh, I will." Paige assured her with a smile.

As soon as Mrs Frazier ambled out the door, Paige threw her pencil down and leaned back in her chair and laughed out loud. *Just wait until Sally hears about this one,* she told herself.

Glancing at her watch, Paige noticed it was twelve-thirty. *No lunch for me today,* she mused to herself. Walking quickly to Sally's office, she stuck her head around the corner and said, "Hey, friend, I can't make it to lunch today. Mrs. Frazier just left and I need to work on her molds, plus some others." She rolled her eyes upward. "Missing yesterday put me way behind."

"That's all right," Sally replied. "I needed to run some errands anyway. Maybe tomorrow?"

"We'll see," Paige said with a laugh. "I don't think you realize how much I have to do. I'll be in the work-room all afternoon if you need me."

Paige was halfway down the hall when she heard a breathless Sally call, "Wait a minute, Paige! I forgot to ask you how your session with Mrs. Frazier went?"

Paige smiled. "Well, for once, things went as smooth as silk." Her eyes sparkled. "Just wait till you see what else she wants me to make her. It'll blow your mind."

"Don't keep me in suspense. Can't you tell me now?" Sally pleaded in a teasing manner.

"No way!" Paige retorted mischievously as she turned her back to her friend. "You'll just have to wait and see."

Sally's eyes danced. "I'll get even!" she exclaimed.

Paige spent the rest of the afternoon in the workshop making the molds from her designs. As chief designer, she was responsible for bringing the design into ex-istence. But she always went a couple of steps further and actually created her design in wax. She used a hot wax pen to carve and work the wax until it was the exact replica of the piece of jewelry on the sketch pad. When the mold dried, she took the actual stones and placed them in the wax model. After this step was completed, she always called the client back in to view her handiwork. If the client was happy with the work, then the model was put through the casting process and the design was created.

Once the mold was made, she turned it over to the tool craftsmen in the workshop, and they put it through the casting machines. From there the piece of jewelry was polished to a dazzling sheen and, last but not least, the stones were set. Paige was thrilled every time one of her creations came to life.

For an independent jeweler, Wallace Jewelers had the best and latest equipment for making jewelry. The workshop was located at the Galleria store where Paige spent the majority of her time. At least two days a week, however, she went to the other stores and designed jewelry for their customers. But all the actual work was carried out at the Galleria workshop, where Paige had a good rapport with the craftsmen. They admired her ability and listened to any suggestion she might have regarding any piece of jewelry.

Her artistic ability, combined with her flare for creating the unusual, brought people from all over the city to sample her talents. She had definitely helped to put Wallace Jewelers on the map. She was proud of what she had accomplished. She wanted people to not only wear her jewelry, but to treasure it as well. She felt she had reached her goal, and didn't hesitate to pat herself on the back every once in a while.

By the time Paige left work that afternoon, it was five-thirty and nearly dark. Shivering from the chill in the air, she unlocked her car and hastily stationed herself behind the wheel. For a moment she sat motionless before starting the motor. She dreaded going home and wished she were back at her own apartment. Her mother would more than likely start in on her once again about her failure to obtain help from Lane. She simply wasn't up for another encounter of this type. The time was long overdue for her to move back to her apartment. Tomorrow she would pack her bags. Having made that decision, she felt much better.

The traffic to her mother's house on West University Place was horrendous. She hadn't been thinking straight or she wouldn't have left the store so early. The bout with Lane had apparently affected her more deeply than she realized. She felt strangely disoriented. During the last two years she had thought of herself as a sensible career woman who could handle anything thrown in her path. Now she wasn't so sure.

All her problems seemed insurmountable. Depression, she thought, was a monster with many tentacles ready to wrap around her, to strangle her. Lane had a way of rousing it to life and leaving her with no weapon to fight it.

As she turned the car onto her mother's street, she saw a strange car parked in front of the house. Her heart lurched. The car was big, long, expensive and threatening. It had to be Lane's. No one in Katherine's circle of friends drove a Lincoln Continental.

Panic gripped Paige. Katherine! No telling what her mother was saying to him about their troubles. The thought of it repelled her.

Swerving her car into the driveway, she let the motor idle for a moment, thinking. She could, if she chose, jam the car in reverse and disappear. But running scared never settled anything.

With a grim expression on her face, she switched the ignition key to off and methodically closed and locked the car door. *Remember,* she scolded herself mercilessly, *he doesn't want you. He* never really did. *For once, be strong, Paige Morgan!*

Breathing deeply, she walked the last few yards to the front steps that led up to the entrance. She pressed her lips together, turned the knob and pushed open the door. She took off her coat and flung it aside, not bothering to look to see where it fell.

She looked up to see her mother appear in the doorway that led to the den. Katherine looked anxious and unsure of herself.

"Lane's here," she said unnecessarily, indicating the room behind her. "He's just arrived and is waiting to see you." She hesitated. "How was your day?"

Paige was aware that her mother was making small talk to cover the awkwardness of the situation.

"My day—my day was fine," Paige finally muttered, although somewhat absently, but her thoughts weren't on her work. She quickly checked her hair to make sure the matching combs were still secure and glanced down at her skirt, blouse and sweater vest to make sure all was intact. Her face was devoid of color, so she pinched her cheeks.

Katherine remained where she was, eyeing Paige with puzzlement mirrored on her face. "Do you...do you want me to leave you alone with Lane?" She lowered her voice to a confidential whisper. "He was barely civil to me," she finished in a petulant tone.

At this point Paige didn't want to be alone with Lane. But having her mother hovering nearby wasn't the answer either. She felt like a trapped animal. Permitting none of these thoughts to reflect on her face, she allowed Katherine to step aside and let her walk into the den.

Lane was standing by the fireplace with his arm resting on the mantel when she entered the room. The soft glow of the lamplight highlighted to perfection the male beauty of his body. Her senses heightened as she noticed how vitally attractive he looked in his dark brown pants and cream-colored velour sweater. Her eyes absorbed the sight, dwelling on the broad, muscular sweep of his shoulders.

"Paige," he inclined his head politely.

Tension crackled in the air as he watched her like a panther stalking its prey. Paige could feel her mother hovering nervously in the background.

"Coffee?" Katherine suggested, her confidence returning. "I know you'll want a cup, Paige. How about you, Lane?" She paused waiting for his answer.

"That sounds fine, thank you, Katherine," Lane returned in a formal and abrupt tone.

Paige saw her mother's lips tighten. But Katherine, for once, held her tongue and hastily departed toward the kitchen.

From sheer weakness, Paige lowered herself onto the couch, completely avoiding his gaze. She waited for him to speak, still avoiding looking in his direction.

With a lithesome smoothness, Lane crossed the room and sat down beside her on the couch. His weight compressed the cushions, making it impossible for her to keep her distance. She fought for a stationary position to keep from touching him. She stared pointedly out the window at the darkening street. The warm ends of his fingertips gently grasped her chin and turned her around to face him. Her eyes flared wide.

"Paige," he murmured, peering deeply into her blue orbs "why did you run away from me yesterday?" His breath caught in his throat. "I can't believe you hate me so much that you won't even talk to me."

The smoldering darkness of his gaze had its usual effect on her. Like a child, she couldn't move or speak. *If I didn't know better,* she thought, *I would swear there was pain and hurt in his voice.*

When she finally found her voice, she replied rather unsteadily, "Because…"

"Because why?" he repeated softly, never removing his eyes from the fine-boned beauty of her face.

She didn't know what to say. Breaking the spell, she rose abruptly, her body stiff. Her control was slipping. His attempt to placate her with tender looks and soft words infuriated her.

Not bothering to hide the contempt she harbored, she said between clenched teeth, "Why did you come here this evening?" She paused, looking at her watch. "I'm sure you have other commitments."

He pointedly chose to ignore her last comment and replied to the first, surprisingly without rancor. "You know why I'm here."

She managed to maintain a cool front. "You're wasting your time and mine," she replied. "Just forget I ever came to your office and leave me alone."

He made a weary gesture and tried another approach. "Have you had anything to eat?"

"No," she answered impulsively.

"Good. I haven't either." He paused, uncurling his large frame and rose from the couch. "We can continue this conversation over a nice hot meal."

She panicked. "I'm not going anywhere with you, Lane." Her voice was unsteady.

Before she realized it, they were facing each other—both tall, both determined, both inflexible.

"Yes, you are," he ground out, his voice edged with steel.

Paige closed her eyes. No way would she do it. She wasn't even going to leave this room with him.

Stalling for time, she clenched and unclenched her fingers. "I'm sure my mother has already told you what you wanted to know, so why the pretense?" She was aggravating him, but she couldn't seem to stop herself.

He lifted innocent brows. "I'm sorry to disappoint you, but your mother told me nothing." He paused, the lines deepening around his mouth. "I wouldn't have let her tell me, anyway. Katherine and I have nothing to say to one another." His voice was laced with bitterness.

Paige grew puzzled. Lane seemed to have changed his opinion regarding her mother. Or maybe she was letting her imagination run away with her. Maybe

Lane just blamed her whole family for her having left him.

Pushing these thoughts aside, she turned toward him with a softer look on her face. "Please, Lane..." She paused, groping for the right words to impart her feelings. "Won't you just go? I seem to be repeating myself, but I can't seem to make you understand we have nothing to say to each other any more." She chewed her lower lip. "After all, you're getting what you want—aren't you? So why do you even care?" There was anger in her voice as well as a kind of defiance.

His eyes darkened. "You are *still* my wife." His words had an ominous ring to them.

"But thank God not for long," Paige snapped. The second she uttered the words, she knew she'd made a mistake.

A dark color swept up to Lane's hairline. He uttered a vicious expletive and stepped toward her in a threatening manner. Her words had aroused him. But at that moment, her mother chose to enter the room with a tray of coffee. The silence grew strained as Paige made her way back to the couch and weakly sat down.

Katherine, sensing all was not well, began pouring the coffee in a subdued fashion. "Cream and sugar?" she asked hesitantly, looking at Lane.

"I'll take it black," he answered abruptly, shifting his gaze once more to Paige. Paige ignored him as she took the cup from her mother's outstretched hand. She sipped it quickly, grasping the cup as if it were a life-line.

Lane didn't sit down but instead strode over to the

fireplace and positioned himself there once again. He seemed to lord over them all, Paige mused bitterly.

The swarthy cast of his features was clearly outlined—the firm line of his chin and the tautness of his jaw line. No doubt about it, he was still angry and was striving for the control he had momentarily lost.

When Paige felt her nerves were at the breaking point, Lane broke the strained silence. "Paige, get your coat," he said tersely. "We're going to grab a bite to eat." Calmly, gracefully, he walked over and placed his coffee cup on the tray in front of Katherine. "Thanks for the coffee, Katherine. It was nice to see you again," he finished in an aloof tone.

Although her mother wasn't completely attuned to the undercurrents in the room, she nevertheless understood Lane was on the verge of being rude. She flushed, but again held her peace and merely said, "It's nice to see you again, too."

Paige was really puzzled now. Again there was the veiled contempt aimed at her mother. She truly didn't understand why Lane was vindictive toward Katherine. Before she and Lane separated, he had always indulged both her mother and her brother to the point of spoiling them. It always seemed to give Lane pleasure to do things for both of them, especially from the material standpoint. Her mother eventually came to expect these "necessities" from Lane, and it was a bitter pill to swallow when all these pleasures ceased with the breakup of their marriage.

She felt Lane's eyes on her, waiting quietly for her to do his bidding. She was incensed. "I'm not leaving this house with you," she declared sharply. "I told—"

His eyes glittered dangerously. "Either you go with me now or you can have the pleasure of my company for the entire evening. It's your choice." There was a veiled threat in his tone. He meant every word he said.

Swallowing hard, she glared at him. "Oh, all right! If that's what it takes to get rid of you..."

"Paige," he warned, his nostrils flared, "you'd best mind that sharp tongue of yours."

She caught her lower lip between her teeth to keep it from trembling. With a defeated sag to her shoulders, Paige made her way toward the hall closet and grabbed her coat. She almost laughed hysterically at the look on her mother's face. Katherine's eyes, big as saucers, kept bouncing from one to the other as she sensed the volcanic tension between the two of them. Her mother would, Paige had no doubt, let her sacrifice her life for her "darling Jamie."

Paige didn't ask where they were going as Lane propelled her out of the house and helped her into the car. After making sure she was comfortable, he went around to the other side and settled himself behind the wheel.

There was a loud silence between them as Lane guided the vehicle with his competent hands. Paige sat with her own hands knotted tightly in her lap. She could feel Lane's glance on her tense features from time to time, but she refused to acknowledge it. Paige was aware she was behaving completely out of character.

Breaking into her thoughts, Lane asked, eyebrows quirked, ''Do you have any preference as to where we eat?''

''No,'' she returned, pulling the visor down to glance at herself in the mirror. She had been so upset at having to go with him, she hadn't even bothered to make sure her lipstick and hair were intact.

''You look fine,'' Lane announced, a husky pitch to his voice.

She turned to look at him and took in his profile etched against the shadowy darkness of the car. The stereo vibrated soft strains of one of the latest hit songs, and the aroma of his expensive cologne penetrated her senses and sent a warmth coursing through her body. She groaned inwardly. Even though she was loath to admit it, he still had power over her womanhood.

Shortly, Lane guided the car into the parking lot of a new and unique restaurant called Bennigans. When they entered, Lane requested a booth, and they were escorted to one in a secluded corner. Instead of taking the seat opposite her, Lane eased his large frame into the booth beside her, lightly brushing her breast as he did so. She forced herself to remain still and swallowed the gasp that threatened to erupt at his contact.

Not one flicker of emotion crossed his face as he began to study the menu. But then Lane had always been good at hiding his thoughts. When the waiter arrived shortly, Lane ordered one of the house specialities for himself and Texas nachos and a spinach salad for her.

Turning, he asked, "Would you like something to drink?"

She hesitated for a moment. "Yes, I believe I'd like a glass of Chablis." Maybe it would help to settle her nerves, since they were stretched to the breaking point.

"And you, sir?" the waiter asked, looking intently at Lane.

"Better bring me a beer. Whatever you have on tap will be fine." With a nod, the waiter disappeared.

Noticing how closely Paige was backed against the wall, Lane inclined his head slightly and held her gaze. "Would you be more comfortable if I moved across the table?" There was a hint of mockery in his voice.

Paige flushed, looking away. "Perhaps I would be."

He interrupted with a short laugh. "I get the message…" With those words, he proceeded to get up, but not before he sideswiped her thigh with his. She felt the muscles sear her flesh through her clothes. Her face colored as images of their legs and arms wrapped around each other after a night of making love, brushed across her mind and played havoc with her emotions.

Paige prayed he couldn't read her mind.

After their drinks had been served, he said in a grave voice, "Paige, I know you're in some kind of trouble."

She didn't reply.

He paused for so long that she finally lifted her eyes. "Are you pregnant?" he asked with bold rudeness.

Outrage boiled up in her throat! She couldn't believe what she had just heard. Stunned, she finally found her voice, and hissed, "Why, why, you miserable... Of all the insulting—"

Hot tears filled her eyes as she groped blindly for her purse. She had to get out of there, get as far away from him as possible. In her eagerness to leave, she accidently flung her purse against the corner of the table causing it to fly open, its contents spilling on the floor. A sob rose in her throat as she dropped to her knees.

Lane stooped immediately and grabbed her hand and held it close within his own. He groaned raggedly as he said, "Paige, I'm sorry. I don't know what made me ask that..." He paused, as if searching for the right words. "It's just that you made me so damn mad yesterday when you ran out on me." He drew an unsteady breath before continuing, "I was worried—I imagined all sorts of things. Will you accept my apology?"

Her legs quivered. She felt sick to her stomach. With her hand pinned in Lane's large one, she realized that for the moment she was trapped. Struck by the pallor of her skin and the trembling lower lip, Lane gradually began to relax his hold on her hand.

"You can let go now," she said in a dull voice. "I'm not going anywhere."

Time became meaningless as together they collected the strewn contents of her purse. She realized, once she was again seated, that the only way all this agony was going to end was for her to tell Lane about Jamie. It didn't matter anyway, since she wouldn't accept his help now, even if he offered it. The very idea of him thinking that she might be pregnant with another man's child while still married to him was almost more than she could bear.

Knowing that he had at least won a reprieve, Lane grew less tense and leaned back into the thick cushion of the booth.

But Paige wasn't fooled. If she made the slightest move toward the door, he would stop her. He sat coiled like a rattler, ready to spring at a moment's notice.

Running a hand tiredly over her eyes, she said in a listless voice, "It's Jamie, Lane. He's the one in trouble, not me."

Lane showed no surprise. "As always," he commented dryly.

Paige plucked at her lower lip. "It's difficult to know where to begin—"

"From the beginning," interrupted Lane. "Go on, I'm listening." His softened tone gave Paige the confidence she needed to continue.

When she had finished recounting every detail of her brother's latest escapade, she waited for his explosive reaction. But there wasn't one. He merely leaned forward and said, his expression veiled, "It's a hell of a mess, I'll admit." He sighed. "I'm not promising anything, understand, but I'll see what I can do, especially about the California thing."

"Don't bother," she returned coldly. "I don't want your help. Not anymore."

Lane refrained from saying anything because the waiter arrived at that moment with their dinner. The sight of it made her stomach feel worse than ever.

However, she forced herself to take a few bites, and drink a little more of her wine after the waiter refilled her glass.

Because she hoped this was the last time she and Lane would be together, she had to ask him one question. She hesitated for a moment, watching him as he sliced his steak, before she said, "Since I've answered your question, suppose you answer mine."

His eyes darkened as he nodded. "That seems fair enough. Fire away."

Paige swallowed the lump in her throat. "Why, after all this time, are you suddenly wanting a divorce?" She drew in her breath. Now that she had asked, she wasn't sure she wanted to know the answer.

Lane looked at her intently. "I'm in the process of closing the deal on a very important merger for controlling stock in another jewelry store chain." He paused, holding her gaze. "Any type of scandal, such as a divorce, would have jeopardized my chances of successfully completing the deal."

She moistened her suddenly dry lips. "I see." She spread her hands. "Well! I guess that takes care of that!"

Lane's eyes became guarded. "There is one more reason."

Paige stared at him as her heart skipped a beat. "Well?"

He frowned, as he took a sip of his beer. "I've found someone else I want to spend the rest of my life with." His eyes narrowed speculatively on her face, waiting.

Without flinching, Paige said, "Who is she?"

"Does it really matter?" he asked, his tone soft.

"No, but I want to know anyway." Paige felt as if she was on stage, acting out a part.

Lane heaved a sigh. "Her name is Jill Taylor. And she's interested only in me and a family, and not in a career."

A knife twisted in her stomach. How *dare* he sit there and say those untruths to her! *If only he knew the truth,* she thought bitterly. She wanted to lash back at him, but that would only succeed in hurting her more. She must keep reminding herself that he cared nothing for her and never had.

The thought of him with another woman didn't bear thinking about. *If only we could go back,* she grieved. Their marriage had been perfect at first. Even now, as angry as she was, if he touched her and said he was sorry, that he wanted to start over and make it work, she would listen. But she knew that could never be, too much had gone beforehand—too much pain, too many unkind words and too much sorrow.

Not bothering to linger over coffee, Lane asked for the check. The trip home was made in strained silence, each lost in thought.

Lane drew the Lincoln to a halt in front of her mother's house. After seeing her safely inside the door, he said softly, ignoring her mutinous expression, "I'll be in touch."

Her throat was too tight to speak. After she locked the door, she leaned her back against it and gave in to her tears.

Four

Before Paige left for work the following morning, she and her mother had another argument concerning Lane and Jamie. It was at that point that Paige informed Katherine she was moving back into her apartment after work. Her mother wasn't pleased with that turn of events either, but she could see that Paige was adamant and wasn't about to change her mind.

She had plenty to keep her busy at work, but thoughts of Lane and their evening together kept intruding. The pain and bitterness were uppermost in her mind, but she was loath to admit, even to herself, the attraction she still felt for him. She wanted desperately to deny it, but in all honesty she couldn't. Her weakness bothered her immensely, making her feel like the kind of woman she despised.

She promised herself she wouldn't think about Lane and another woman. And she wouldn't think about divorce. She had work to do, and she would put last evening out of her mind. What she felt for Lane wasn't love anymore, anyway; it was sex, pure and simple. To care for him after all this talk of divorce was demeaning. But when he had accidentally touched her, it had made her long for more.

The possibility that she might still be in love was ludicrous. She wanted to end the marriage as badly as he did.

During the rest of the day Paige kept her fingers crossed about Thomas. Perhaps he would come through with a decent lawyer who could defend Jamie without charging her a small fortune. She dreaded calling the family friend, so she kept postponing it. But Jamie had to be found, and time was scarce. She needed help soon.

In order to keep her sanity, she chose to sketch a piece of jewelry that was complicated as well as costly. Through registered mail that morning she had received a large quantity of pear- and oval-cut diamonds in various weights. She eagerly began work on a design which would complement these stones to the fullest. After destroying sketch after sketch, she finally came up with what she thought was a beautiful pattern. She chose to use the stones in a necklace shaped in a circlet of flowers. The petals, containing the smaller round diamonds, would be laced at the back, and gradually the diamonds would become larger and the pear-shaped ones would be in the front. Each petal mounted in platinum was to have approximately seven stones. She planned to cut the molds tomorrow, and, barring complications, the necklace would be in the showroom case shortly thereafter. She was positive it would only be a matter of days before the piece sold.

She was tempted to work on Mrs. Frazier's cockroaches, but with her disturbed thoughts, she decided against it. It was a quiet day around the store. Ron had flown to New York and had taken Sally with him, leaving Paige and the sales clerks all alone.

By the time she arrived home, it was six o'clock and she was totally drained. After she let herself into her apartment, she went immediately to the bedroom and dumped her two small suitcases on the floor. Paige then took a quick survey of her kingdom. It was good to be home, she mused to herself as she eyed her surroundings, making sure nothing was different.

Although her apartment was small, she thought it had charm. The living area was furnished in wicker with green and orange seat cushions and pillows. Wicker baskets filled with plants occupied various corners, creating a cheery effect.

The remainder of her homey abode consisted of a tiny compact kitchen, a small dining nook with a wicker glass-topped table and chairs to match, a bedroom and petite bath. She lived only minutes from the Galleria, which enabled her to get to work without having to fight the horrendous Houston traffic.

Since her separation from Lane, she had made her home the center of her life. She hoped, though, that with her new position and raise, she would be able to afford a larger apartment, but only if she didn't have to go too heavily into debt to get Jamie out of trouble.

Each time the problem of money crossed her mind, she instantaneously thought of the jewelry Lane had given her. At present, it was in a safety deposit box at the bank. Although there wasn't a lot of it, what she had was valuable. She was averse to the idea of cashing it in for money.

Pushing these rather disturbing thoughts aside, Paige made her way to the kitchen to check the contents of the refrigerator, or rather, the absence of contents. She grimaced to herself. It served her right for not stopping at the grocery store on her way home, but she had been too tired. She resigned herself to another dinner of crackers and cheese.

Before she could even contemplate relaxing, however, she went downstairs to get her mail. The thought of what awaited her there made her insides churn.

She bit her lip as she jerked open the door and made her way to the mailbox. Just as she opened it, Mrs. Lowery, the manager, stuck her head out the door of her apartment and smiled at Paige. "Oh, hi," she said. "I see you finally made it back. Are you here to stay for a while?"

A sigh escaped Paige. "Yes, ma'am, I certainly hope so. It's nice to be home again." As she conversed, Paige scanned her mail and noticed that the one item she was looking for was missing.

She frowned. "Mrs. Lowery, did the postman by any chance leave any of my mail with you? It's apparent my box couldn't hold anymore mail and I'm missing..."

"Ah, yes," Mrs. Lowery interrupted, "As a matter of fact he did. Wait just a minute and I'll get it for you." She turned around and disappeared into her apartment. A moment later she returned with a bundle of mail encased in a rubber band. "Here you are, my dear." She smiled. "The postman asked about three or four days after you'd gone if he could leave your excess mail with me.'' She paused to catch her breath. ''I didn't think you'd mind.''

Paige smiled, shaking her head. ''Of course not. I'm sorry I didn't make arrangements to take care of it before I left.'' She smiled again before continuing, ''I really appreciate your taking care of me. Thanks a million.''

''You're welcome. I was glad to do it.''

Paige slowly began moving toward her apartment. ''Well, I'd better get back upstairs. I have tons of things to do. I'll see you later.''

She knew from past experience that Mrs. Lowery would talk her head off if she remained any longer. She was a dear, but she loved to gossip more than anyone Paige had ever known. And Paige wasn't about to satisfy Mrs. Lowery's curiosity concerning her whereabouts or her business.

The minute she closed the door behind her she dropped down onto the couch and ripped open the envelope from Lane's attorneys. Sure enough, there was a curt note from *him* as well as several pages of papers requiring her signature. She leafed through them rapidly before stuffing them back into the envelope. Hot anger surged through her body.

Her hands trembled and her mouth went dry. He wanted a divorce? Then he would get his divorce. Why prolong the inevitable? Why wait three months? Why not go to Las Vegas and get a ''quickie'' one? Lane would certainly agree with her. After all, he could marry his intended much sooner that way.

The shrill sound of the telephone ringing jolted

Paige out of her frustrated reverie. She reached over to the end table and quickly grabbed it, practically shouting into the mouthpiece, "Yes?"

"Paige...is that you?" a velvet-edged voice questioned.

Her pulse accelerated! She clutched the receiver tightly. "Yes, it's me." Her voice sounded hostile.

She heard his intake of breath through the phone. "I was checking to see if you were home. How long have you been there?"

"Long enough," was her curt reply.

"I see...." He sighed heavily.

She had to end her torture once and for all. Licking her dry lips, she said, "Lane—I've been thinking..."

"So have I," he interrupted with a note of brightness in his voice. "But first I want to let you know I've hired a private detective to try and locate Jamie. I know how worried you are..."

"You did what!" she cried. "I told you I didn't want your help."

His tone hardened. "I *know* what you said, but..."

"There are no buts about it!" She paused, switching the receiver from one ear to the other in nervous agitation. "I aim to take care of Jamie myself. I've been doing it for two years—remember?" She continued quickly before she lost her nerve. "I've come up with an idea I'm sure you'll find agreeable. I see no reason to wait the three months for a divorce. Let's just fly to Las Vegas and..."

Another sharp intake of his breath halted her in midsentence. He then said in a taut voice, "Paige, you are the most infuriating and exasperating woman I know! I'm offering to help find your teenage brother who has run away and is in Lord only knows what kind of trouble. And what are you doing? Well, I'll tell you. You are obsessed with your pride, your humiliation and your own feelings!''

She couldn't believe his outburst. "I see no point in continuing this conversation." Her voice quivered in spite of her effort to keep it under control.

"Nor can I," he hissed, "and the more I think about it, the better I like your idea of a quick divorce. I'll talk to you later!''

With those words, Lane abruptly and loudly hung up on her.

Paige sat staring at the receiver in her hand for a few seconds before replacing it in the cradle. She was stunned at his words as well as his actions. Why was he taking the trouble to try and find Jamie? Surely a man who wanted nothing else to do with her wouldn't take the time to involve himself with her family's problems.

However, Lane had always been an honorable and fair man and had truly cared about Jamie and had wanted the best for him. She was positive the only reason Lane wanted to help was because he *was* concerned about her brother. His feelings for her, one way or the other, probably never entered into his decision at all. If she could just keep that analysis in mind, everything would be all right.

Paige was relieved that she no longer shouldered the entire responsibility of finding Jamie. Hunting for her brother on her own could have proved more than she was capable of handling. Her mother would be ecstatic on learning that Lane had taken matters into his own hands.

After forcing down the cheese and crackers, she poured herself a Coke and headed for the shower. She let the hot water relax her body until she felt a little of the tension fade away. She then crawled into bed, hoping that sleep would come as soon as her head hit the pillow. Unfortunately, she tossed and turned all night, dreaming. She dreamt she and Lane flew to Las Vegas and stood before a cold hostile judge who treated them and the multitude of others waiting for a divorce like a herd of cattle—as if they were all less than human. It was unbelievably degrading...

Paige woke up at five o'clock the next morning, her pillow moist with tears. As she sat on the side of the bed, she tried to clear her head of the awful nightmare.

Breathing deeply to calm the uneasy feeling in her stomach, she made her way to the bathroom and splashed her face with cold water. She was shaking violently and hurried to turn up the central heat, knowing full well this wouldn't relieve her discomfort. She wasn't dealing with her problems like the level-headed, mature woman she had been. She needed to get hold of herself.

Ignoring breakfast, she forced down two cups of coffee and hastily dressed for work. She dialed the time and temperature and, learning it was 40 degrees, decided to dress warmly in a wine-colored gabardine skirt, and a long-sleeved matching velour sweater.

She applied more makeup than usual in order to hide the dark circles haunting her eyes. They were becoming a habit and drew too many questions from her co-workers. She wasn't in the mood for any soul-searching questions, especially from Ron. He and Sally were due to be back in the store following their quick trip to New York.

The instant Paige walked into her office, she picked up the phone and called her mother. Of course, Katherine was delighted when Paige told her Lane was going to help find Jamie. She tried her hardest to get all the details out of her, but Paige remained aloof and told her mother only what she needed to know.

Paige worked on designs all morning. She postponed calling in clients to examine their preliminary molds. She wasn't up to embarking on that laborious task, so she contented herself with sketching several items for the salon. Ron had been after her to do this for some time and she was finally getting around to doing it.

She was so preoccupied with what she was doing that she failed to notice Sally standing in front of her desk until her friend coughed.

"Whatever you're working on must be something special." She grinned impishly. "It's not Mrs. Frazier's special design by any chance?" Sally leaned over the desk, pretending to look.

Paige laughed. "Sorry to disappoint you, my friend, but I haven't even started on Mrs. Frazier's 'special design' as you call it." She paused, brushing a strand of loose hair out of her eyes. "I'm finally getting around to working on several pieces for the salon, instead of doing one at a time. The front showcase is practically depleted and Ron's been on my back.''

Sally's mouth turned down, ''Well, I wish you'd hurry with Mrs. Frazier's. I'm dying of curiosity.''

Paige rolled her eyes. ''Patience, patience,'' she said, grinning. ''Remember it's a virtue.''

Changing the subject, Sally quipped, ''Can you make it to lunch today?''

Paige sighed, shaking her head. ''No, I can't.'' she glanced down at her watch. ''I'm due at the downtown store in about forty-five minutes to meet a client.''

Sally frowned, her eyes serious. ''When *are* you going to have some time for us to get together?'' She paused momentarily. ''Have you talked to Lane anymore?''

Paige averted her eyes. ''Yes, I have.'' She knew there wasn't any need to gloss over the truth. ''Actually he's hired a private detective to find Jamie.''

''Whew!'' Sally exclaimed. ''When he sets out to do something he does it in a big way.'' Her face puckered. ''But...how did he find out about Jamie? I thought you didn't tell him...''

''I didn't, then,'' Paige interrupted, ''but I've talked to him since, and he took matters into his own hands, as usual.'' Her tone had a bitter edge.

Sally hesitated. ''Is the divorce still imminent?''

Paige's lips thinned. ''As soon as possible, if I have my way.''

Sally expelled a sigh. ''Well as far as I can tell,

relations between you two haven't improved. Am I right?''

"One hundred percent!" Paige retorted. Hot tears threatening to spill and, refusing to break down again in front of Sally, she removed her briefcase from the drawer and began stuffing it with her designs. She was acting like a fool, sniffling every time the word *divorce* was mentioned.

If Sally sensed that Paige was upset, she refrained from acknowledging it. Instead she stated, sliding off the desk, "I'd better get back to work."

Paige stood up and smiled. "I have nothing planned for lunch time tomorrow. How about you?" She paused, waiting for Sally's answer.

"Sounds fine to me," Sally chirped. "Gotta go now. I'll talk to you later."

As Sally headed toward the door, Paige said softly to her retreating back, "Thanks for caring. I..."

Sally playfully put her hands over her ears and, turning swiftly, shook her finger at Paige. "Paige Morgan, if you thank me one more time, I'm..."

Paige laughed, throwing up her hands. "Okay, okay. You've made your point. My lips are sealed from now on. I promise."

Paige stood still for a moment after Sally left. Sighing, she donned her coat, grabbed her briefcase and left. As she drove toward her destination, it dawned on her that Ron hadn't come to the office. If she'd thought about it in time, she could have asked Sally about him.

All I can think about, she thought bitterly to herself,

*is Lane Morgan—his compelling personality, his pow-
erful arms, his overpowering masculinity and his all-
consuming touch.*

The only way she could relieve herself of these ex-
cruciating thoughts was to immerse herself in her
work. Work was good medicine; it exhausted her mind
as well as her body.

She kept up her pace of hard work throughout the
week. The time, however, passed at a snail's pace. She
and Sally kept their lunch date the next day and had
a good time visiting with each other. Sally related the
latest details concerning her love life and had Paige
laughing until she cried. Lane wasn't mentioned, since
Paige had nothing new to report. But they did discuss
Ron—his continuing absences and his violent temper
of late. They agreed that something was wrong, but
neither could suggest a cause for his odd behavior.

Every time the phone rang at home and at the store,
Paige flinched inwardly. It was never Lane. She wasn't
expecting any news of Jamie this soon, but she was
anticipating some word from Lane saying arrangements had been made for the trip to Las Vegas.

By Friday afternoon, her nerves were frayed. As she
let herself into the apartment, she kicked her shoes off
and sank down onto the couch. She had no desire to
even read her mail. Finally, she went to her room and
discarded her clothes for a robe and slippers.

She wasn't hungry, but made her way to the
kitchen, nevertheless, to make a small dinner. She decided to have a ham and cheese omelette and a slice

of toast. Lane used to love her omelettes and she fixed them for him often. Her stomach muscles tightened at the memory.

Having lost her appetite, she had to make herself eat. The fluffy egg mixture tasted like sawdust in her mouth. After cleaning up her mess, she walked toward the bathroom. A good hot shower was what she needed before she climbed into bed.

She was untying the sash on her robe when the phone rang. She hurriedly went to answer it. Her heart beat quickly as she picked up the receiver and said, "Hello."

"Are you busy?"

"Oh, hi, mother," she answered, letting her breath out slowly. "I was about to step into the shower."

"I won't keep you long, then," Katherine said in a dejected tone. "I only wanted to know if you'd heard anything."

"No," Paige replied, her tone gentle. "You know I'll call you the minute I do."

Katherine sighed. "Are you by any chance coming over this weekend?"

Paige hesitated. "I wasn't planning to. I have a lot to catch up on around here…"

"I understand…" her mother began, her voice taking on a martyred note.

"But I'll call you," Paige cut in, "probably tomorrow and Sunday too."

"All right. I'll talk to you later then. Bye."

"Goodbye," Paige said and hung up the receiver.

She felt a twinge of guilt plague her. Her mother

was distraught and lonely and she should probably go and see her. But she couldn't bear the thought of another confrontation. She had a lot on her mind and desperately needed some time alone.

After her shower, she put on a pair of nylon lounging pajamas and curled up on the couch with a paperback bestseller. Her hair remained piled on top of her head and her face was devoid of makeup. She was totally relaxed and looked forward to a good night's sleep.

She was so engrossed in her book that the melodious sound of the doorbell didn't even penetrate her thoughts. However, the insistent clarity of it finally pierced her consciousness, causing her to grimace. She glanced at the kitchen clock as she untangled her legs from under the afghan and leisurely made her way toward the door.

"Who is it?" she questioned hesitantly.

"It's me, Lane."

She remained motionless.

"Paige, for God's sake, open the door. It's colder than hell standing out here."

Still in a stupor, she reached for the dead bolt and slowly opened the door, standing aside for him to enter. She quickly slammed it shut as the cold damp air caused her to shiver.

"It feels great in here," Lane exclaimed as he began removing his coat. She noticed his eyes as he surveyed her apartment. "Nice," he mused, casting a warm gaze in her direction.

Paige turned her head, but not before her eyes took

in the deep lines carved around his mouth and the tired angle of his shoulders, as he removed his coat.

The silence continued as she remained where she was, clinging to the doorknob for support. After swallowing hard, she managed to stammer, "Are…are you here about Jamie or…or the divorce?"

Anger hardened his lean features. "Yes, to the first and no, to the second," he ground out tensely.

Her fingers curved into a ball.

"Damn, can't I even sit down and get warm before the inquisition begins?"

Paige flushed. "Fine," she stated, "go ahead, make yourself at home." The sarcasm dripped from her voice as she uprooted herself from her place by the door.

His clean manly smell still clung to him, instantly permeating the whole apartment and causing her further discomfort. Her eyes, like magnets, rested on his tired features.

Lane's only reaction to her show of sarcasm was to clench his jaw as he lowered his frame onto the couch. "Am I ever beat," he muttered, rubbing the day's growth of beard on his chin. A sigh of pleasure escaped his lips as he leaned his head back against the cushion and closed his eyes.

Paige was close enough to see the thick eyelashes as they fanned against his upper cheeks. How many times had she planted butterfly kisses across those very same eyes and…

"Would you care for something to drink?" she

asked abruptly forcing her thoughts back to reality. "Coffee?"

"Please...if you don't mind."

He looked exhausted and she found herself weakening toward him once again.

"How about something to eat as well? Maybe an omelette?"

"No, thanks," he said as he opened his eyes and turned to stare at her for a timeless moment.

He was the first to avert his gaze. "I stopped for a hamburger a little while ago." Although his tone was husky, the spell was broken.

Paige nodded and escaped to the kitchen where she busily set to work measuring the coffee. As her hands performed this task, she treated herself to a further perusal of him. He looked tired, vulnerable and lost. His condition pulled at her heart strings.

Her legs were unsteady as she carried two cups of coffee on a tray and set it on the table. The noise aroused him, causing his eyes to flutter. He smiled. "I didn't mean to barge in and then expect to be waited on."

She returned his smile with a watery one of her own. "That's all right." She paused, nibbling at her lower lip. "What's your news of Jamie?" she questioned hesitantly.

He sighed. "I flew in from Belgium this afternoon, and when I arrived, there was a message to call Jim." Seeing the question in her eyes, he backtracked. "I'm sorry—Jim is the private detective I hired to find Jamie. Anyway, I returned his call and he wanted a detailed description of your brother and a recent photograph. I gave him the description but I don't have a picture..." He paused, breathing deeply. "He wants it first thing in the morning."

Paige looked away. "I see..." Now was a good time to bring up the divorce. Why was she stalling?

His mouth twisted. "Is that all you can say?"

"No, no, of course not," she stammered, wetting her lips. "It's just that I'm not sure I have a recent enough picture here..."

"Well, whatever you can come up with will have to do," he shrugged.

She nodded. "I'll be back in a minute, then." Her legs were still a little unsteady as she got up and moved quickly to the bedroom.

Paige was rummaging through the top drawer of her dresser when she felt the hair on her neck stand on end. Turning swiftly, she encountered Lane leaning negligently against the door frame, his tie askew. There was an unreadable expression in his eyes.

"Need any help?" he asked huskily.

"No...I finally found what you wanted."

The photo was clutched tightly in her hand as he strode toward her. "Here, let me see." His tone was gentle.

As he came nearer, Paige halted him at arm's length by stretching her hand outward with the picture exposed.

Lane slowly took it from her and slipped it into his shirt pocket. His eyes remained firmly glued to hers—probing, questioning.

Even at arm's length, he was too close. His rugged and unkempt appearance had an appeal all its own. Paige swallowed hard. She couldn't move.

His eyes seemed to be memorizing her face as they roamed from the shimmering brightness of her eyes, to the perfectly chiseled nose, and came to rest on the haunting sweetness of her lips. He leisurely raised his index finger and traced the outline of her mouth. She was powerless to stop him. His finger traveled down her swanlike neck to the swelling fullness below.

His finger didn't still, but continued its wandering—searching, seeking the delights of her womanhood he remembered so well.

To her regret—the search stopped. He slowly dropped his hand.

Paige couldn't breathe. She was completely captivated by the beguiling sweetness of his touch.

The ripeness of her body was molded to perfection within the confines of her apparel. It was obvious that she wore nothing underneath.

Her breathing quickened and with it her breasts rose and fell in a steady rhythm. Lane could see the outline of her nipples through the fabric, like rosebuds, small and pointed.

"Oh, God," he whispered, lowering his head. "I'll hate myself for this tomorrow, but I can't help..." He pressed his lips fiercely against hers. She responded immediately as his tongue probed the inner richness of her mouth. A flame rose in her as she returned his fiery kisses. They devoured one another with their lips, their tongues.

It was Paige who finally regained her senses when she tasted the salty tears that mingled with their passion.

She pulled away, almost causing them both to lose their balance. She fought for air and composure. Lane too, was having a hard time. His breath, when he drew it, was rugged. And the white line around his mouth had deepened.

Finding her voice, she managed to say, "I...I think you'd better go..."

He stared at her for what seemed like an eternity, then turned abruptly on his heel. The firm click of the front door was the only sound in the apartment.

Sleep took a long time coming that night. She wasn't able to cope with the longings his wandering hands and kisses had aroused in her. She had wanted more. Her body was in a shambles and she was powerless to help herself. She wanted Lane with an all-consuming desire that frightened her. And it wasn't just sex; it went much deeper than that.

For a moment he had wanted her. But the words that he uttered kept coming back to haunt her. "I'll hate myself tomorrow...I'll hate myself tomorrow..." There had been bitterness and sadness as well as passion interwoven in the strangled words.

For the remainder of the weekend, Paige stayed in limbo. She washed her clothes, cleaned her apartment and even called her mother. All of these duties were performed automatically and without any feeling.

The days passed. There wasn't any word from Lane

concerning Jamie or the divorce. Her mother was frantic and Paige had her hands full coping with her. In spite of everything, Paige still trusted Lane when it came to finding Jamie. He would stick to his word. She consoled Katherine as best she could and with each new day, she buried herself further in her work.

During that time, she created a few stunning pieces. Her favorite was a pair of diamond dewdrop ear clips with a matching ring. They were exquisite and sold within an hour after being placed in the showcase.

Another of her favorites was a 3.21 carat marquise-cut natural blue diamond set in a platinum mounting with thirty-one baguettes surrounding it. She called it a ballerina ring.

She finally had an opportunity to work on Mrs. Frazier's special design. She experimented with various ways to make cockroaches into pierced-ear studs and necklace. She decided to obtain real cockroaches and pour hot wax over them, creating a perfect mold, knowing that Mrs. Frazier would be delighted when she presented the idea to her.

Sally was almost beside herself upon learning what the store's "favorite" customer wanted. "Now I know she's nuts," she had said, throwing her hands up in hopeless despair.

Paige had laughingly rejoined. "Remember—different strokes for different folks." But even with her increased activities, time passed slowly for Paige. She had reached a point of dreaded uncertainty.

She was encased in utter despair as another weekend approached. Ron tried to get her to go to a party with him, but she refused. He hadn't been pleased about being turned down. His temperament hadn't improved either. She caught him staring at her on numerous occasions with a brooding expression on his face. Until he got his problems straightened out, she wanted as little as possible to do with him.

Paige awakened on Saturday morning with a distinct feeling of apprehension. The obnoxious ringing of the phone beside her bed merely added to her misgivings.

Hesitantly she reached for it, saying more sharply than she intended. "Hello."

"Paige?" She heard Lane's voice, loud, clear and concerned.

"Yes," she responded quietly.

"Are you all right?"

"Yes—I'm fine. I was sleeping..."

"Well, I'm sorry to disturb you at this hour, but you need to get up and get dressed. We found Jamie and we have to go get him."

Paige sat straight up in bed. "Are you serious? Is he okay?"

"Now calm down," he commanded in a smooth tone. "He's just fine. We have quite a distance to cover, so hurry—okay? I'm on my way."

She jumped out of bed and threw on a pair of designer jeans and a sweater. While she waited for the water to boil for some instant coffee, she called her mother. Katherine was ecstatic when she heard the news.

By the time Paige sat down with her coffee, her energy was spent. With a few quiet moments, however, she began to think...

Jamie had been found and would soon be home. Her stomach jumped at her next thought. The divorce...

Five

The knock on the front door startled Paige. Hurriedly she grabbed her purse and coat and opened the door.

Though casually dressed in a pair of slacks and sweater, Lane looked as if he belonged on the cover of a men's magazine. His clothes molded his powerful physique to flawless perfection.

A smile alighted his features. Seeing her face pale, Lane frowned. "Is something wrong?"

"No—no, not really." She hoped he couldn't read her mind.

He cocked his head to one side and said, "Well, then, if you're ready, we need to be on our way. Jamie's in Austin, so we have a hard three hours' drive ahead of us."

Paige was astounded. "What on earth is he doing in Austin?"

Taking hold of her arm and ushering her down the stairs, Lane said, "As soon as we get in the car, I'll fill you in on all the details—okay?"

Paige quickly removed her arm from his grasp and halted. "Lane," she protested, "there's no need for you to go clear to Austin. I can do it myself."

He firmly steered her in the direction of his car.

"Paige, do you always have to be so damned stubborn? I'll drive you. I'm not asking now, I'm telling."

She nodded blankly and soon found herself in his plush Lincoln Continental. She was glad Lane hadn't argued with her. Even though her words sounded brave, she wasn't sure she was capable of going after Jamie alone. As Lane lowered himself into the seat beside her, he immediately stretched his long muscled arm across the seat, reaching for something in the back. His thigh slid next to hers and remained there while he continued his fumbling. His touch was like an electric current shooting through her body.

His eyes probed hers for a moment. His control, too, had slipped. Before she could analyze his expression, the familiar mask fell into place and he was once again the impeccable Lane Morgan.

He reached for the ignition key, but not before he dropped a small brown package in her lap.

"What's this?" she asked, looking down at the envelope and then up at him with a puzzled frown on her face.

"Just hold on to it a minute and then I'll tell you. First things first. I want to tell you about Jamie."

"Please do," she replied bleakly.

Softening his expression, he said, "I don't know any gentle way to break this to you." He paused, obviously searching for the right words. "Jamie spent the night in jail in Austin."

Her eyes widened. "In jail! But, but...how? Why?" She spread her hands. "I don't understand..."

"Now take it easy. It's not as bad as it sounds."

He paused, holding her gaze. "Jim called me early this morning and told me he had tracked Jamie to Austin and did I want to go after him? Of course I said yes. No charges have been filed yet and as soon as we get there, he'll be free to go."

Paige let her breath out slowly. "But why did they pick him up?" she cried. "You haven't explained that."

His eyes narrowed. "Actually, he was found asleep on a park bench about midnight last night. Jim got a lead on his whereabouts last night and called the authorities in Austin this morning thinking they just might have him, and sure enough they did."

Paige linked and unlinked her fingers. "What now?" she managed to ask through a tight throat.

"I'm not sure at this point, although I can tell you that this latest escapade won't help his case in court one bit. In fact, it'll just add fuel to the fire for the prosecuting attorney. He's going to need one hell of a good lawyer to get out of the mess he's gotten himself into."

Paige felt cold inside. "I simply don't understand why he ran away." She shook her head. "It's beyond me. But kids nowadays are just different..."

He shrugged. "You've answered your own question. Young people, like Jamie, have had too much, too soon, and some are unable to cope. In your brother's case, he had it all and then abruptly lost it along with all discipline and supervision."

"I guess you're right," she said, expelling a sigh.

"I know I'm right," he returned with a granite hard expression on his face.

Her insides were in utter chaos as she turned and gazed out the window as the miles raced by. The sky, with its threatening thunder clouds hanging overhead fitted her mood perfectly.

How would she cope with this new development concerning her brother? Jamie's being picked up by the law, as Lane had pointed out, made everything more difficult and complicated. Now that Jamie had been found, Lane would most likely place the responsibility back in her lap entirely.

She felt certain Lane rued the day she came back into his life. Turning in her seat, she glanced at him; he probably had blocked everything out of his mind except the road. It had begun to drizzle, making driving more hazardous. He was such a skilled driver that she never feared placing her confidence in him.

His hands, as they gripped the wheel in a relaxed but controlled fashion, were long and tapered, their gentleness capable of reducing her to putty.

Hot tears filled her eyes. She kept her head averted and blinked them away. She must be strong throughout this ordeal. She wanted Lane to be with her, to take care of everything. She was so deep in self-pity that when Lane placed his hand over hers, she nearly jumped.

"Sorry, I didn't mean to startle you," he intoned huskily. "I know you're doing nothing but brooding and it won't accomplish a thing."

"I know, but..." she replied in a near whisper.

He squeezed her hand. "Shush! I don't want to hear it!" His voice was cajoling. "Trust me—mmm?" He lifted her hand and placed it beneath his on the steering wheel.

She could only nod. Her voice was too full to speak. She kept her eyes glued to the back of his hand, seeing the black hair sprinkled there and feeling the warmth crawl up her arm from his touch. Maybe he didn't intend to desert her, at least not right away.

Lightening the mood, he grinned and nodded toward the package, releasing her hand at the same time. "Go on, open it. It won't bite, I promise."

She smiled as she began fumbling with the string wrapped around the tab, and heard his warm chuckle as he watched her struggle. She shot him an agitated look, but his smile merely broadened. Finally she managed to get through the string and tape to the contents of the package. She was stunned as she peered inside and saw the—diamonds!

There were loose stones of every size, cut and weight. Although she had handled a lot of stones, her excitement mounted at the rare quality of these gems.

"Go on, pour them out," he urged, smiling.

Needing no further persuasion, Paige dumped the contents of the envelope in her lap, closing her legs tightly to keep the diamonds from falling through. She was still in awe at their sparkling beauty. She never tired of looking at, handling or working with the treasures in front of her. Each one, no matter how small or large, had its own mark of exquisite elegance.

Their love of precious stones had been a strong attraction between them and still was. During their years of married life, they loved to discuss this subject for hours at a time. Even now with all the differences that existed between them, there remained this common ground on which to communicate.

"Where on earth did these come from?" She smiled at him, her face relaxing a little.

His eyes twinkled. "I brought them back with me from Belgium a few days ago."

"But why?" she asked, her brow furrowed in puzzlement. "Surely you aren't in a habit of carrying this type of cargo with you?"

He gave a short laugh. "Hardly," he acknowledged. "But these little jewels"—he paused, scooping up a handful and then letting them slowly trickle out of his hand back into her lap—"are the very first ones to be cut in my new factory in Antwerp."

Her eyes widened. "I didn't realize it was in operation."

"Then you do know about it?" he inquired raising his eyebrows.

She shook her head. "Only what I read in *Jewelers' Magazine,* which wasn't much." She grinned, casting her eyes sideways. "Plus a little gossip through the grapevine, of course."

"Oh, of course," he mocked her humorously.

She flushed. "Well, you know how it is when you get to be rich and famous."

His eyes darkened. "I hope you don't believe everything you read," he said in a clipped tone.

She stiffened. "Not all of it..."

''Well, don't,'' he said, cutting her off sharply.

There was a taut silence.

Paige bristled inwardly. They couldn't seem to be in each other's company very long without a sparring match taking place between them. She had only been teasing him about the gossip, but apparently she had struck a raw nerve.

Until recently, she had avoided any publicity connected with Lane—gossip as well as newspaper articles. Maybe if she *had* paid more attention, she might have learned about his lady friend and wouldn't have been so shocked when he had asked for the divorce.

The silence between them deepened as the miles swept by, and the drizzle turned into a bleak, steady rain. To break the taciturn quiet, Lane reached over and turned on the radio. The beautiful strains of classical music instantly sounded throughout the car's interior.

With an unconscious movement, Lane adjusted the waist of his slacks. He had begun to feel the long miles of driving. He shifted his weight and, glancing at her without warning, caught her staring at him.

His brows lifted. ''Something the matter?''

Paige wrenched her eyes away and blindly riveted her gaze to the windshield wipers. ''No, I mean...no, nothing's the matter.''

She wondered what Lane wanted from her. Did she dare hope or think he might be using Jamie as an excuse to see her? She chastised herself; how could she think that when they couldn't even carry on a decent conversation for more than five minutes without one or the other inflicting verbal abuse?

Forcing these uneasy musings aside, Paige let the music and the hum of the car's engine lull her into a deep sleep.

She was halfway awakened by the gentle caress of a hand against her cheek. She unconsciously sighed and snuggled up against it.

It was Lane's deep-throated chuckle, followed by his seductive words that quickly brought her back to reality. "My, my, little kitten, if I had known how a little rest was going to affect you, I..."

Her eyes flew open as her face flushed with color. In a confused voice she asked, "Where are we?"

"At the police station in Austin."

His words had a sobering affect on Paige. She blinked her eyes in rapid succession hoping to orient herself.

His piercing gaze remained on her.

She felt the color drain from her face when she realized her blatant action of a moment ago. She couldn't look at him as she fumbled for her purse.

An amused grin came to his firm lips as he got out of the car and walked around to open her door. She was still mortified by her actions and ignored his outstretched hand, getting out of the car on her own.

As they walked the distance from the parking lot to the station, Paige felt her heart begin to thump. She abhorred the thought of her brother being in jail and not knowing where it was all going to end.

She was glad of Lane's firm hand on her arm, guiding her up the steps. As her legs began to falter, his hold tightened and they entered the huge swinging doors.

Paige fought for courage as they made their way to the sergeant's desk. She felt desperate to at least try to handle the situation. It was unfair of her to lay the entire responsibility for securing Jamie's release on Lane's shoulders.

Before Lane could say a word, Paige stepped closer to the sergeant's desk. The sergeant raised his head and stared at her. No emotion crossed his face as he asked in a bored tone, "May I help you?"

Paige cleared her throat. "Yes, I'm..."

He interrupted impatiently, "Are you here to pick up someone?"

"Yes...yes," she stammered, "Jamie McAdams."

"Are you his guardian?"

Paige flinched inwardly at his abrupt manner. To make matters worse, he seemed to look through her as if she weren't real.

"No...I'm his sister. I..." Her voice faltered.

Quickly, she turned her tear-filled eyes to Lane—pleading, trusting. He was standing beside her. He stared at the man in charge for a long moment.

Then, in a cold, firm voice he said: "My name is Lane Morgan. Please get on the horn"—he paused, indicating with a motion of his hand the telephone on the sergeant's desk—"and send for Jamie Mc-Adams."

From that moment on, the following hours were

hazy ones for Paige. It was as if she were a bystander watching from afar.

The red tape involved in securing Jamie's release would have been endless for Paige. But Lane took care of everything. Even though he was dressed in casual clothing, his air of authority influenced the people around him.

When Lane and one other officer finally escorted Jamie into the room where she waited, Paige felt her eyes slowly fill with tears.

Her brother looked bedraggled and forlorn. But it was his physical appearance that caused Paige to gasp. He was thin to the point of being gaunt. His skin clung to his bones, his blond hair was dirty and uncombed and his blue eyes were listless and dull.

Since his youngest teenage years, he had never allowed his mother or Paige to show him any physical affection at all. But now, seeing the lost look mirrored on his face, she took a hesitant step toward him. A tear rolled down his hollow cheek before he moved. They met halfway. With a sob, Jamie threw his arms around Paige, clutching her tightly.

With the tears cascading down her face, Paige held him and soothed him as best she could. When his anguish had somewhat abated, it was Lane who untangled his arms from around Paige and in a gentle voice said, "Come on, son. Let's go home."

Spending a night in jail had left its mark on Jamie. He was totally exhausted. The moment he settled himself comfortably in the back seat of the car, he fell sound asleep.

Paige wanted to ask Jamie why he ran away. She wanted the answers to many questions. But Lane shook his head at her, anticipated her thoughts. "Let him sleep. It's the best and quickest healer of all. We'll question him later—together."

Together. It had a pleasant ring to it, raising Paige's downtrodden spirits. But she mustn't read too much into what he said. He had made no promises for tomorrow and she really expected none.

As the Lincoln Continental sped down the highway back toward Houston, each was lost in his own thoughts. Again, the haunting sound from the stereo flowed in and out of Paige's mind as she tried to dispel the gloom that had settled upon her slim shoulders.

The further west they traveled, the harder it rained. It took all of Lane's concentration just to keep the car on the road.

From time to time, the radio announcer cut in and gave a weather update. His voice droned on and on. "Travel advisory in effect for north Texas, northeast Texas and parts of south Texas.... Rain mixed with sleet and snow is expected, making bridges and overpasses extremely hazardous.... Please limit all travel unless absolutely necessary.... Another bulletin in half an hour. Now back to smooth music for your listening pleasure..."

Paige sighed inwardly as she lay her head against the soft velour of the seat and let the music soothe her troubled thoughts. She was overwhelmingly conscious of Lane's nearness—the aroma of his cologne that still clung to him and the muscled thigh which often brushed against hers. She closed her eyes hoping to close her memory as well.

"Paige...are you asleep?"

The softly spoken words penetrated her drugged senses. She sat up and turned toward him.

"No," she answered briefly.

"Do you mind doing me a favor?"

"Of course not," she responded, unconsciously moving closer.

"Could you get my pipe and tobacco out of the glove compartment and pack the pipe?"

Feeling the color recede from her cheeks at the memory his request evoked, Paige opened the glove compartment.

After she finished filling the bowl of the pipe with tobacco, she watched as he took his lighter and the tobacco caught fire.

"Thanks," he murmured simply, after having taken several satisfied draws.

"You're welcome," she returned in a near whisper.

Paige couldn't believe how easily he asked her to prepare his pipe. It had been a favourite habit they shared. One of those "wifely" duties she had performed so lovingly, so long ago.

The deep silence settled between them once more as the miles sped by. Lane intruded briefly to ask if she wanted to stop for anything to eat. She shook her head and retreated into her shell of conflicting desires and thoughts.

The further they traveled, the more time she had to study this enigmatic man beside her. This man, who was still her husband, but in name only—who had, at times today, acted as a real husband. He had protected her, cared for her and had fleetingly shared a treasured moment of the past with her. But what she held most dear was his physical presence. He was here beside her. He hadn't deserted her. Somehow, that helped to ease the pain of the past and the future.

Finally, Lane pulled the car into the driveway of her mother's house. They were hungry and tired, except for Jamie, who had slept during the entire trip.

After turning off the ignition, Lane reached over and tapped Jamie on the leg, rousing him. "You're home."

"Already?" the sleepy-eyed teenager moaned.

"Yes, already," repeated Lane softly.

Jamie blinked his eyes several times. "I...I...want to thank..." He broke off, shame masking his features. He lowered his eyes and began fumbling with his duffle bag.

"Son," replied Lane gently, "look at me."

Jamie lifted trusting blue eyes to meet Lane's dark ones. "Don't worry about thanking me with words. You can thank me by conducting yourself like the respectable man you are from now on. Is it a deal?"

Jamie shook his head vigorously, obviously too choked up for words.

A small smile broke across Lane's features and he again lightly brushed Jamie's knees. "Let's go in, son. Your mother's waiting."

Once inside, Katherine immediately wrapped her arms around her son in a bear hug which he only halfheartedly returned. Was the sullen expression she was so used to seeing creeping back into his face? Paige hoped not as she looked closely at her brother.

The next hour at her mother's house was an extremely draining one for Paige. She sensed that Lane didn't fare much better.

Immediately after cooking Jamie something to eat, Katherine started arguing with him. Paige tried to interrupt, but was bluntly told to stay out of it. At this point, her mother's hysterical antics only made Jamie more belligerent and confused. They never once learned why he ran away, nor could Katherine make him promise not to do it again.

When Lane had had his fill of Katherine, he stepped in, sending Jamie to his room with a promise of talking to him later. Turning toward Katherine, he said in a cold, controlled voice, "Berating Jamie in that manner isn't the answer. You can't put your arms around him and pet him one minute, and turn around the next and box his ears. Can't you see what you're doing?"

Katherine's lips thinned but she refrained from saying too much to Lane. She was aware that he was totally responsible for Jamie coming home.

Shortly thereafter, Paige and Lane were about to walk out of the house when her mother said, "Oh, by the way, Paige, Ron has been trying to get hold of you. He's called here several times. He wants you to be sure and call him."

Paige ran a hand tiredly over her eyes. "Did he say what he wanted?"

Katherine shook her head. "No, just that message."

Paige shrugged her slim shoulders. "Well, thanks for telling me. I'll call him later..."

After being settled once more in the car, she shuddered from the cold and pulled her coat more tightly around her as she waited for the heat to seep into her bones. It was not only cold and damp, but the sky was now threatening sleet. As Lane drove the car up the ramp leading to the Southwest Freeway, he turned toward her. "How well do you know Ron Wallace?" His tone was dry.

Her eyes widened. "Why do you ask?"

He shrugged. "Just curious, that's all."

Paige was positive it was more than mere curiosity that made him ask that question. But she knew it was pointless to say anymore. She could tell by his tightly clenched jaw that he had said all he intended to say on the subject.

Before she realized it, Lane had pulled in front of her apartment unit. He got out of the car and walked around to help her out. This time she didn't ignore his hand, and together they quickly ran up the steps to her door.

What now? Should she invite him to come in? She couldn't believe herself—here she was acting like a dewy-eyed teenager on her first date instead of a twenty-five-year-old woman who'd been to hell and back.

They stood apart, oblivious to the cold, each waiting for the other to make the first move. She began fumbling in her purse for the key, stalling.

When Lane turned, as if to walk away, Paige spun

around toward him, catching her lower lip between her teeth. "Would you like to come in for some coffee?" She clutched the key tightly in her hand.

"Only if you want me to," he said cautiously.

Her only answer was to hand him the key and move aside for him to open the door.

The warmth of the room enveloped them as they stepped into the entry. Lane immediately offered to help Paige with her coat. As he stood behind her, he said close to her ear, "Did I ever tell you how much I like your apartment? I could completely lose myself here."

"That's exactly what I do," she replied, a trifle unsteady. His warm breath on her neck ignited her senses and made coherent speech almost impossible. Her entire body was afire as the spark raveled to the lower regions of her stomach.

Paige hastily moved in the direction of the hall closet to hang up her coat. Lane also removed his, choosing to drop it over the nearest chair.

Looking back at him over her shoulder, she remarked, "I know you must be hungry." She paused softly. "Do you have time for me to fix you something to eat?"

"Thanks, honey, but no thanks," he responded in a gruff voice. "I'm too tired to eat."

"I know the feeling," she agreed. "It's been a long day."

He rested his eyes on her pale face, taking in the dusky circles under her eyes and the weary droop of her mouth. "How about a cup of hot chocolate? If you'll go sit down, I'll be glad to fix it."

She flashed him a sweet smile. "That sounds nice, but I'll do it. After all, you did all the driving—as well as everything else," she finished tremulously.

His eyes narrowed into a lazy, measuring look as he covered the short distance between them.

Her nerve endings quivered as his hand reached out and gently stroked her face. His touch was delicate, almost imaginary. But the feelings it evoked were very real. She ached with unfulfilled desires. For two years she had repressed all her physical wants and needs. *What he is inflicting on me is unfair!* she cried to herself in utter despair.

Paige bent her head forward to keep him from seeing the confusion and pain in her eyes. Her hair, with unknowing sensuality, tumbled about her shoulders.

She heard the rugged intake of his breath. "I...ah, I think I'll fix that hot chocolate." He strode into the kitchen without looking at her.

Her head spun around and her mouth was too dry for her to speak. She silently complied with his earlier command and made her way on shaky legs to the couch.

She rested her head against the back of the sofa, forcing all thoughts from her mind. It did no good to think. She kept asking the same questions over and over and had yet to come up with any answers.

She jumped nervously when she felt the cushion next to hers sink downward. She could feel the heat radiating from his body as he leaned his head back against the cushions. She sat perfectly still, afraid to breathe, afraid to move, and felt the hunger for this man race through her blood like poison.

Paige felt rather than saw Lane as he turned toward her. In slow motion, he reached over and turned her head to face him. Their eyes met and held as if a spell had been cast upon them. Paige couldn't control the rapid beating of her heart.

Lane's breath caressed her face as he said, "What about your hot chocolate? It's getting cold." His voice was husky with emotion.

She tore her gaze away from his and reached for the mug. "I...I almost forgot about it."

Her hand trembled as she lifted the mug toward her mouth. But she never reached her destination. Lane gently withdrew the cup from her hand and set it down on the table.

She held her breath as he moved to begin softly fingering her hair, playing with an errant curl before locking the silky strand behind her ear. He outlined the tiny lobe exposed to his gaze with gentle fingers and then replaced his finger with his tongue, nibbling until she nearly cried aloud.

When he sought her mouth, she offered no resistance. His tongue ran lightly over her lips, and she sighed, opening her mouth. Everything inside her was melting, drowning, as she wound her arms around him, locking him tight, racing headlong through a maze which had no end. His kisses were excruciatingly moist and tender as his tongue sparred with hers, seeking the sweetness of her mouth.

Their lips still joined, he slowly pressed her back against the softness of the cushion where he now had free access to the other delights of her body.

"So lovely," he murmured as he tore his mouth away from hers for a second. "All softness."

The palm of his hand was massaging her breasts until she felt the nipples strain against his touch, demanding more. His lips molded once again to hers as his hand traveled under her sweater. The front fastening of her bra was immediately released by his warm groping fingers.

She heard him sigh against her lips as he teased first one nipple and then the other with his fingers. When Lane was no longer satisfied with that, he inched the sweater upward until her breasts and swollen nipples were exposed to his mouth. As his tongue and teeth tugged and caressed each one, she felt the burning sensation spread to the lower regions of her stomach. She wound her hands in his thick wiry hair, encouraging him to love her as only he was capable of doing.

They were completely lost in their loving when the telephone pealed loudly, jarring the mood.

"Let it ring," Lane rasped, as his mouth relinquished her nipple.

"No," gasped Paige, "I've got to answer it."

"No, you don't," he countered.

The phone couldn't be ignored. It kept ringing until Lane, fighting for his breath, nearly knocked it off the table as he groped for the receiver. "Yes," he barked loudly into it.

After a few seconds, he slammed the menace down.

The sound exploded in the quiet warmth of the room like a bullet hitting a tin can.

Striving for composure, Paige sat up and in a dazed and uncertain voice whispered, "Who was it?"

Lane turned pain-filled eyes toward her and rasped, "Would you believe a goddamn wrong number!" He slumped forward and buried his head in his hands...

Hot tears filled her eyes as she jumped up from the couch and walked toward the window. She pulled the cord, opening the draperies—anything to occupy her hands—and gazed out into the inky blackness of the night.

Out of the fog, she heard Lane say huskily "Paige."

She turned on him like a tiger. "No!" she hissed. "Don't you dare say one more word to me."

"Paige, please..." His voice held a pleading note.

"No!" she cried once again. Paige felt the heat rise in her throat like hot bile. Swallowing hard, she turned and gave him a cold and indifferent look.

With hunched shoulders, he met her stare with a grim look in his eyes.

"I want you to promise you won't come here again—ever." The silence that followed these words allowed Paige to continue. "I don't know what kind of game you're playing but..." Again she paused, breathing deeply. "But, whatever it is, I don't intend to be a part of it any longer."

Lane, rising to his feet with an expletive, ran a hand around the back of his neck and walked into the middle of the room. "At least give me a chance to explain," he demanded harshly.

"Please—please, don't," she implored, turning her back on him. She felt her hard-won composure slipping. "I'll sign the divorce papers tomorrow and send them to your lawyer, without fail."

'Dammit Paige, would you just listen!"

Ignoring his outburst, she went on, "You can do as you like about the divorce—a quick one or—or whatever..." Her voice had narrowed to a dull monotone.

After a moment, she went on, breaking into the harsh silence. "Every time you called or came by, I kept waiting for you to bring up the divorce again. But you never did. Now it no longer matters one way or the other. I just want you out of my life."

After uttering those last words, Paige turned and looked at Lane. He took a step toward her, but stopped dead in his tracks when he saw the expression on her face. He was struck by the pallor of her skin and the tears edging her eyelashes.

The soft glow of the lamplight gave her a haunting ethereal look. But the proud defiant set of her shoulders left no doubt that, in spite of the pain, she was in control.

Lane's throat tightened. *What have I done to myself?—to her? How could I betray myself like this?*

When he finally spoke, his voice was low and held the same sadness and trace of bitterness she had noted before. His attitude was strange, yet oddly arousing. "If it's any consolation to you, I deem myself the world's biggest fool." With that he was gone.

Once more Paige was left with nothing but her memory, her pain and a hollowness within...

Six

Two weeks later, at exactly one hour after closing time, Paige laid her pencil down and rubbed her weary neck and shoulders. She couldn't remember ever having been this overworked. She had pushed herself almost beyond repair, and it was beginning to tell on her. She had lost weight, which she didn't have to spare; the dusky circles under her eyes had darkened; and she was irritable and short-tempered.

She and Ron had reached a strange impasse. At a time when they normally would have been working closely together, he persisted in skirting any issue which might bring him in contact with her. Paige, not knowing what to do, avoided him. Sally stayed away from them both. Sally had tried to talk to Paige—about Ron, about anything—but nothing anyone said or did penetrated Paige's present shell of discontent and unhappiness.

The only bright spot in Paige's life was Jamie's behavior. He had apparently gotten his act together and was behaving as he should have all along. But Paige and Katherine couldn't take the credit for his attitude; that accomplishment belonged solely to Lane.

After they had returned from Austin, Lane visited

Jamie, unbeknown to Paige for several days, and the two of them had their counseling session. Lane had once again, she discovered, kept his promise concerning her brother.

She kept thinking that the harder she worked, the easier it would be to sleep at night. But nothing seemed to free her mind. One moment she berated herself for her actions and the next moment she ached for Lane with an intensity that was overwhelming.

She hadn't heard one word from him since she had signed the divorce papers and returned them to his lawyer. She could only assume that in the near future she would be a free woman.

Paige had totally wrapped herself in a cloak of pain and remorse. She lowered her head on the desk, cushioning it with her arms. The neck massage had helped immensely and she thought that now she might be able to make it home.

She didn't know how or why, but she sensed all of a sudden that she was no longer alone. Her heart flew to her throat. It wasn't time for the janitorial service to come and clean. Surely, Ron or Sally had locked the front door when they had left?

Afraid to move or look up, but more afraid not to, Paige cautiously lifted her head.

Lane leaned indolently against the frame in the doorway to her office. The expression tightening the lines about his eyes was angry.

"What the hell are you doing staying here after closing time with the door unlocked? Aren't you aware that someone could come in and steal everything in this place, not to mention what they'd do to you?''

Paige was speechless, first with the shock of seeing Lane standing in front of her and second, because he had attacked her so unexpectedly.

When she finally found her voice, she stammered, ''I—I had no idea the door was left open. It's never happened before.'' She paused, rubbing a hand over her tired eyes. ''If I'm not mistaken, Ron was the last one to leave. I find it hard to believe he would leave the front door unlocked.''

''Well, the ignorant bastard sure as hell did. When I laid my hand against the glass with the intention of tapping it in order to get your attention, the door gave way under my hand. As you can see, I walked right in.'' His voice was accusing.

Paige flushed. Although she realized his temper wasn't altogether directed at her, she nevertheless caught the brunt of it. She wasn't in the mood to be yelled at or talked down to. Why was it that every time she saw him she was in a predicament?

In a clipped tone he said. ''I don't ever want you here again after closing time if your *boss* isn't any more responsible or concerned than to do something stupid like that.'' He thrust his hands deeper into the pockets of his pants as he strode to her desk and perched himself on the edge of it. ''I've never in all my life...''

She'd had enough. Standing up, and seething inwardly, she said through clenched teeth, ''Would you please just be quiet! And while I'm at it, I'll remind you that you don't have the right to demand anything from me.'' Her lips quivered and she immediately bit them. She abhorred the idea of Lane knowing how much he had upset her. However, she ought to be used to it by now, but she wasn't.

She hadn't fooled him. His razor sharp eyes missed nothing. He took in the shimmering brightness of her eyes, the tumultuous curve of her mouth and the turbulent thrust of her chest. The rounded sweetness closeted beneath her silk blouse heaved to show exactly how agitated she really was.

Paige saw his eyes darken, and the pulse raced in his throat. She held her breath as she turned and walked to the file cabinet to get her purse.

She didn't intend to get anything started that neither of them had any intention of finishing. It dawned on her as she opened the file cabinet drawer and reached for her purse that she didn't even know why he had come to her office. Glancing at him out of the corner of her eye, she pretended to rummage through the files.

He had removed himself from her desk and was looking around the office. Although he looked a bit haggard, he was dressed superbly in a dark brown suit with a cream-colored silk shirt and tie to match. Even the well-cut suit couldn't hide the power which emanated from him.

Every time they saw each other, it always ended in bitterness. How much longer could they continue to function under these conditions? She was positive that each time she saw him would be the last time. But he always returned and the explosive tension smoldering between them inevitably surfaced.

His back was turned to her and she noted a somewhat dejected droop to his shoulders. Was he, too, suffering? Why did he continue to torment himself as well as her by not going through with the divorce the quick way?

The only reason she could come up with was the assumption that he knew that he was getting under her skin and that he thoroughly enjoyed seeing her squirm. *Yet, not two minutes ago,* she reminded herself, *he had been concerned for my safety.*

"If you're through wasting time, I'd like to go somewhere and talk." His sharp brown eyes impaled her.

"If it's about Jamie, we can talk here." She took a deep breath. "If it's not, then I can't see that we have anything else to say to one another." She averted her eyes as she slammed the drawer shut with a solemn bang.

He made a weary gesture. "If I give you my word I won't touch you, will you come with me to my apartment?"

She raised her eyebrows in alarm, shaking her head at the same time. "No—no, that's not possible. The only thing you could possibly have to talk to me about is Jamie. And you can say whatever you have to say right here!"

His mouth straightened into a firm line. "No, I can't," he expelled harshly. "I gave you my word I wouldn't touch you. What I have to say is important and best said in more comfortable surroundings." He paused, dragging his palms down his thighs. "Anyway, I'm tired and haven't eaten and you look as if you could stand a square meal yourself."

Paige flushed at the veiled insult he threw her concerning her appearance. She was aware she looked as if a truck had run over her, but his accusation made her angry.

She felt raw and exposed. Shivering, she wrapped her arms around her body as if to shield herself from his piercing eyes and sharp tongue.

Paige began chewing on her lower lip. Could she trust him to keep his word? She couldn't stand a replay of their last two encounters.

She was due to meet tomorrow with a lawyer she had enlisted through Thomas. She was worried about the cost of his legal expenses and was panicked over the situation. She intended, however, to see it through, no matter what the cost.

Lane sensed she was weakening and continued trying to persuade her. "Joseph will be there…"

She hesitated, pressing her palms to her hot cheeks. Dare she take the risk? "All right," she acquiesced with a sigh.

Now that he had won, Lane covered the space between them. "I'll get your coat while you close up."

She nodded her head, causing her hair to swing outward and lightly brush his face. She heard the sharp intake of his breath as he quickly turned, putting distance between them. Paige felt hot tears pricking at her eyes.

Before she could change her mind, Lane draped the coat across her shoulders and guided her out, making sure the front door was securely locked behind them.

In the car, the usual silence ensued as they sped toward Lane's high-rise apartment. It had been two years since she had been there. She dreaded returning, knowing the memories it would recall.

She forced herself to take a deep breath and concentrate on the Christmas decorations that lined the city streets and peeped through the windows of the houses they passed. She found it difficult to immerse herself in the Christmas spirit. She had never felt less joyous in her life and hadn't even bothered to decorate her apartment much less shop for any presents.

Her thoughts were interrupted as Lane drove the big car into the underground parking garage. After Lane walked around the car and opened the door for her, they made their way in silence to the elevator.

As Lane inserted his key in the door, the door opened and Joseph greeted them. His eyes widened in astonishment on seeing Paige, before his face broke into a warm grin. "Why, Mrs. Morgan, it's sure a pleasure to see you."

Paige inclined her head with an answering smile. "It's nice to see you, too, Joseph. How have you been? And Marion?"

"We're both just fine, just fine," he said, shaking his head. "Only thing, the arthritis gets us both down every so often, but otherwise we get along all right, for two old folks, that is."

"Well, I'm glad," Paige replied warmly.

As she stepped from the entrance hall into the den, she saw that the room was exactly as she remembered it—the lush mint green carpet, the beautiful draperies but, more than anything else, the overall sense of tranquility and comfort was exactly the same. The view was still awe-inspiring. She crossed to the picture window and stood staring at the twinkling lights of Houston.

She was so caught up in the view before her eyes that she jumped when Lane's soft voice penetrated her thoughts.

"I'll pour you a glass of Chablis and then if you'll excuse me, I'm going to change my clothes." He wearily jerked the tie loose and unbuttoned the top button on his shirt. "I've been going at a nonstop pace since daybreak and I'm exhausted."

Paige lowered her thick eyelashes so that he wouldn't catch her staring at him. After pulling off his tie and stuffing it in his pocket, he crossed to the bar and poured her a glass of wine and opened a cold can of beer for himself.

With an ironic, "Make yourself at home," he sauntered to the bedroom, closing the door softly behind him.

Her shoulders sagged. If only he would say what he had to say and take her home, she would survive. Holding all these pent-up emotions inside was hard on her.

She wished that she, too, was dressed in something more comfortable. However, she felt secure in her serviceable tweed skirt and silk blouse with its matching jacket. She kicked off her high-heeled pumps and nestled her feet in the plush carpet as she eased herself down on the couch to wait for Lane.

As she sat mesmerized by the flames from the wood-burning fireplace, she couldn't help but cast her thoughts on yesterday's memories—especially the good times they had shared in front of the fireplace. Their lives were still entwined, yet so far apart.

Shortly she heard the soft thud of Lane's footsteps behind her, turning, she saw him striding toward her. He had changed into a pair of casual knit slacks and a V-necked long-sleeved sweater. The pants accented his slim hips and the open-necked sweater exposed the dark shadow of his body hair. As her eyes flickered over him, she was hypnotized by his compelling masculinity.

His eyes were dark and inscrutable as they watched her closely. "May I get you another glass of wine?" he asked softly, his gaze never wavering.

"No. I'm fine, really I am." She gathered her scattered wits about her. Seeing him standing in front of her—strong, handsome, so much a part of her in many ways—removed all thoughts of their impending divorce, Jamie's troubles and past pain. For a fleeting moment she wanted to fling herself into his arms.

As suddenly as the thought occurred to her, the absurdity of it overwhelmed her. She rightly viewed it as temporary insanity. This love-hate tug of war was playing havoc with her emotions. She couldn't justify thoughts of this kind, no matter how hard she tried.

"Paige—I," he began in a muffled tone, only to be

interrupted by Joseph bringing in their dinner. Lane ran a restless hand through his hair and walked across to the windows, his shoulders hunched.

She pulled her eyes away from him and made herself pay attention to what Joseph was saying to her. Paige hoped she answered his questions halfway intelligently. But at this point, she couldn't swear to it. Small talk wasn't exactly what she had in her mind.

After Joseph left, Lane seated her at the table that had been set up close to the fire. It was cozy and warm and not at all the atmosphere for thinking about food. She felt her face grow hot at her thoughts, and as a result, she tackled her food more vigorously than she intended.

After dinner they sat down once again in front of the fireplace. The crackling of the fire was the only sound in the room. Then, with a deep sigh, Lane slowly uncoiled his long legs, stood up and walked toward the fireplace. He propped his arm on the edge of the mantel and looked down at her. She met his gaze, waiting for him to tell her why he had brought her here.

"Is Jamie still behaving himself?" he finally asked.

She hesitated. "Yes, as a matter of fact he is. But you know that, don't you?"

He shrugged. "As you say." He paused, as if uncertain as to how to continue, but then took a deep breath and plunged on forcefully. "As I told you on the way to Austin, it's going to take a hell of a lot of money to get Jamie out of trouble." He raised his eyebrows, obviously waiting for her to say something.

She felt her face turn white as she nodded bleakly.

"I'm willing to put up the money for his defense and hire the very best lawyers available to get him off the hook."

Her eyes widened.

"However," he went on emphatically, "Jamie must be kept in line with discipline and parental control. What he did was wrong, but I definitely feel he isn't the criminal the prosecuting attorney is trying to make him out to be. Agree?"

She frowned. "Yes—I agree. But what's the catch—for you putting up the money?" Her face was raised to his in questionable concern.

His eyes narrowed speculatively on her as his voice lowered. "There is something I must ask from you in return."

Her face froze as she groaned wildly to herself. She knew that Lane Morgan never offered anything unless he got something in return.

With sweet venom in her voice she asked, "And just what is that?"

His expression hardened as she realized her sweet-sour question wasn't lost on him. But he didn't hesitate. "I want you to come back to me. The divorce will be postponed, at least for the time being."

The softly spoken words filled the quiet room. With a jerking motion, Paige got up from the couch. "You can't be serious?" she broke out, turning her nails into her hot palms.

His eyes glinted dangerously. "I don't make inane statements, as you well know."

She couldn't believe that he actually expected her to give up the career and independence she had made for herself and return to him just to gain help and money for Jamie.

His top lip curled. "I don't think you're fully aware of how much money it's going to take to get your brother through this trial. Nor do you realize that if Jamie's case is lost in court, your mother could lose everything she has." He stopped and took in her tense expression before continuing. "Remember, the insurance on the car had expired."

She looked at him in disgust as her eyes filled with hot tears. Turning her back to him she asked flatly, "And what do you expect to get out of the deal?"

"You."

Her blood ran cold. She checked the sob that rose in her throat by biting on her lower lip.

She felt cornered, panicked and disbelieving. The worst part of it all was she knew that Lane was right; Jamie was in serious trouble. And she didn't have the money to hire a good lawyer, even if she sold her jewelry.

Refusing to break down in front of Lane, she quickly brushed the tears from her eyes, squared her shoulders and turned to meet his penetrating gaze.

"Well, what's your answer?" he demanded, in a pressing tone. He had no intention of bargaining. It was to be his way—all or nothing.

Lifting her head defiantly, Paige said in a near whisper, "I don't understand any of this conversation." She rubbed a hand across her tired eyes. "Correct me if I'm wrong, but didn't you tell me not too long ago that you had found the woman of your dreams and wished to marry her?'' Sarcasm was evident in her voice. "Now you're saying you want me?" she shook her head in exasperation. "I simply don't understand…"

"Is it important?" he asked softly.

"Of course it's important!" she shot back at him.

He raked his hand through his hair. "I have my reasons…" he sighed.

She gave him a bitter look. "That's no answer and you know it!" She paused, searching his face. "Why do you really want me back, Lane?" Although softly spoken, her words demanded an answer and he knew it.

Averting his eyes, he said, "Let's just say I still find you desirable and leave it at that, shall we?"

Paige sniffed. She knew there was more to it than that. But what? Revenge? Punishment? She realized desire was high on the list—it lay smoldering in his eyes every time he looked at her. But she sensed that he was hiding another reason behind his smooth facade.

She met his eyes calmly. "I'm sorry—but…" She paused gnawing at her lower lip. "There's no way…"

"Suit yourself," he interrupted, shrugging his shoulders.

Paige gasped. "Is that all you have to say?"

He stared at her in silence.

"Surely you would help Jamie without us getting back together. You don't really want me—you said so yourself." She was aware that she was pleading with him but she couldn't stop herself. What if, in her self-ishness, she caused her brother to go to prison? The thought pierced her stomach like a knife.

Lane's words turned her attention away from her torturous thoughts.

"This arrangement will only be for a few months, if that will help you make a decision. You might also keep in mind that I'll be able to help Jamie—really help him..."

Her shoulders sagged in defeat. She slowly turned to face him. Choosing her words, with care, she said, "All right. I'll agree to do as you ask." Her voice held a tremor that she was powerless to conceal. *If only,* she cried to herself, *he would put his arms around me and tell me everything is going to be all right, I wouldn't feel so alone, so desolate, so used.*

He didn't move except to look at her with an un-fathomable expression on his face.

"Now that we've got that settled," he declared, a more relaxed tone to his voice, "there's another matter I want to discuss with you. Actually, I need your help."

Her eyes widened. *Here it comes,* she thought to herself, *the real reason he wanted me to come back to him.*

"Let's have it," she stated in a dull, listless tone.

Lane heaved a sigh. "I hate like hell to tell you this because it further complicates matters." He lowered his thick eyelashes. "Your boss is trying to block my bid for merging with the other jewelry store chain. I want to know where he's getting that kind of money to compete with me.''

"What!" Paige exclaimed incredulously.

Lane's jaws were clenched. "You heard what I said," he expelled harshly.

"But...but he doesn't have that kind of money. Does he?'' she inquired with a mortified look on her face.

"Not to my knowledge, unless he's involved in illegal activities, such as diamond smuggling."

Her eyes flashed. "Now wait just one minute!"

Lane's mouth twisted. "Calm down, I'm not accusing, I'm merely pointing out possibilities."

She frowned. "How can I possibly help you? I know nothing whatsoever about Ron's personal or business affairs. I merely work for him."

"Ah-ha, now there's the key—you work for him."

Paige knitted her eyebrows together. "So?"

He sighed impatiently. "When you're at work, I want you to keep your eyes and ears open for information that you think might help me."

"In other words you're asking me to spy on Ron?" Her voice dripped icicles.

He looked at her in mild surprise. "I wouldn't exactly call it spying, but if that's the label you want to give it, go ahead. Let me assure you I'm on to some pretty solid evidence against him." He halted, looking down at her intently. "If he is involved in shady deals, I don't want you to be a part of it. You know how sticky this diamond smuggling can get."

She tossed her head back defiantly to meet his cool

gaze. "I'm still averse to spying"—she grimaced every time she used that word—"on the one person who befriended me when I needed it the most."

"What's that supposed to mean?" Lane demanded through clenched teeth.

A grim silence settled over the room.

"You know very well what I'm talking about," she replied tautly, "but now's not the time and place to go into all that."

She breathed a sigh of relief, seeing his thunderous expression lighten somewhat. She had almost started something she was not emotionally prepared to handle.

With an indrawn breath covering the quiver in her voice, she said, "Very well, I'll do as you ask. I've been aware for a while now that Ron was in trouble or worried about something. But I'm truly shocked that he thinks he can outbid you for those stores. Can you promise me he won't be hurt if he's innocent?"

"I give you my word."

"Thank you," she said in a near whisper, lowering her head.

Walking over to her, Lane bent down and raised her chin so that her gaze met his dark unreadable eyes. "When we've both fulfilled our obligations to each other, I promise, if that's what you want, I'll let you go, with no strings attached."

His eyes devoured the haunting loveliness of her face and the tantalizing smell of her perfume as he went on to say, "If you choose your freedom, I'll agree to set you up in business—store, merchandise and enough capital to operate it for a full year."

Paige felt hot tears flood her eyes and then trickle one by one down her cheeks.

A slow smile warmed his face as he gently traced a tear from her eyelashes to her trembling mouth. "How's that for striking a fair deal, Mrs. Morgan?" he asked huskily.

The following two weeks were hectic for Paige. Her life had been turned upside down and at times it overwhelmed her.

Although she hadn't seen Lane since the agreement was made, she talked to him daily. He had left almost immediately for London and then had gone on to Belgium.

Christmas was rapidly approaching and the store's business was booming. Paige was kept busy sketching jewelry, trying to keep up with the demand. It always amazed her how many people waited until the last minute to order an intricate and expensive piece.

Work kept her hands and mind busy and left her little time to fret and feel sorry for herself. She was still a long way from being sure that she had made the right decision.

She wondered what Lane would expect from her once they shared the same house. He had made it plain from the onset that he desired her, but she had already made up her mind that she was not going to share his bed.

She had made the decision to return to him as his wife. He had called it "a fair deal." Perhaps it was; he would help with Jamie, she would help with Ron.

Why couldn't he have said, "We'll help each other, then take another look at our marriage?"

Thrusting these disillusioning thoughts aside, she made herself concentrate on the design she was creating. She was about to put the finishing touches on a pin in the shape of a hummingbird. She sketched it with the idea of casting it in yellow gold and filling it with rubies, emeralds and diamonds. This piece didn't require approval, as her client had left everything up to Paige to create and mold for her, completely trusting Paige's good taste.

Although Paige was interested in the project before her, she couldn't keep her mind on it. She rolled the pencil back and forth in her hand for a second, breathing a sigh. Was her discontent due to the fact that Lane was back in Houston and was going to pick her up in a couple of hours? Her heart skipped a beat at the thought. He was taking her out to lunch and then Christmas shopping.

Immediately after Lane had left for London, she had informed her mother and brother that she was going back to him. They were ecstatic. Of course, she hadn't mentioned the price she had to pay. It was better left unsaid.

Sally, too, was happy for her and didn't question the reason Paige had given her—that she and Lane had straightened out their differences and decided to try to make their marriage work. She had refrained from mentioning Ron's troubles to Sally.

She chastised herself once more for letting her mind wander. But her stomach was tied in knots at the thought of seeing Lane again. As a result, her productivity for the morning was somewhat less than she had anticipated.

Finally the hands of the clock crept around to twelve-forty-five. She had only fifteen minutes to get herself ready. She quickly put her project away and made her way to the ladies' lounge to repair her makeup.

As she surveyed herself in the mirror, she felt that she looked her best. Her mahogany brown hair had a glowing sheen to it and her wool knit dress enhanced her slender but full body.

Lane was waiting for her when she walked out of the store at one o'clock. As he helped her into the car there was an awkward moment between them. He was the first one to break the silence with a smile.

Suddenly, her body once again felt the old familiar disturbing sensations. She tried to squelch them as she answered his smile with a watery one of her own.

Shifting his gaze to the rapid pulse in her throat, he asked gently, "Do you have any preference as to where we eat?"

Hot color invaded her cheeks as his eyes wandered lower to rest on the rounded curves of her breasts. She rolled the pink tip of her tongue across her lips. "No—no, it doesn't matter to me. Any place is fine." She tried without success to mask the confusion she felt. Although he wasn't touching her with his hands, she responded as though he were.

"Good," he replied. "I know just the place where

we can get some good chow and not be disturbed at the same time.''

She nodded her head in agreement.

As he guided the car onto the street, Paige reveled in his lean, muscled frame sitting next to her with graceful ease. The sunlight on the crisp winter day caught the gray luster of his hair and made it stand out against his dark features. His relaxed manner told Paige he was completely in charge.

Lane chose one of Houston's best restaurants. It was a new one to Paige, but obviously Lane was well known, since the maître d' recognized him immediately. After being seated off to themselves, they were presented with menus and a wine list and they ordered quickly.

As her eyes roamed the restaurant, they came to rest more than once on a woman sitting across the room. The woman's gaze was locked in their direction every time Paige glanced her way. The touch of Lane's hand on hers caused her eyes to revert back to him. The other woman was forgotten.

''Where are your wedding rings?'' he asked as he caressed her empty finger.

Paige was flustered and he knew it. She tried to pull her fingers out of his grasp and he gave them up with surprising ease, but with a mocking smile on his face.

When she finally answered, it was in a low tone. ''They're at the bank in the safety deposit box.''

''Would you like me to get you a new one, or do you want to get those out of the bank?''

She stiffened. ''I hadn't really thought about it.''

"Well I have," Lane answered, "And I want a ring back on your finger."

She shrugged. "If it's important to you, I'll go to the bank tomorrow."

"Good," he exclaimed.

While the waiter served them, Paige allowed her eyes to turn in the direction of the table across the room, only to find the woman and her companion staring at Lane and her once again.

It was the younger of the two women who drew Paige's curiosity. Turning toward Lane, she said with puckered eyebrows, "There is a woman behind you who is much more interested in what we're doing than anything else. When I tell you it's okay, turn around and see if you know her."

"Forget it," Lane demanded.

It was not so much what he said, but the way he said it, that made Paige aware he knew who the woman was and why she was staring.

Her skin tingled. "Suppose I don't want to forget it?"

Lane's lips thinned. "Since you're determined to know," he paused, expelling a sigh, "it's Jill—Jill Taylor."

"If my memory serves me right, she's the one you had planned to marry," Paige said through clenched teeth.

His face grew shadowed. "That's past history. We have more important things to discuss right *now*."

Neither one had touched the food in front of them.

"Well, I'm not so sure about that," Paige said

tightly. "Your friend Jill is making a beeline for this table."

Suddenly she was unable to stay any longer and imagine the intimacies which had occurred between this woman and her husband. Paige hastily rose. As she fumbled for her bag, Lane's determined hand clasped hers, pinning it to the table. Her head jerked upward, and she saw the lines around his mouth whiten and become taut.

"Sit down, Paige," he said with quiet intensity.

Slowly, she lowered herself back into her chair.

When Lane turned to greet Jill, the shutter was drawn and he was, as ever, the polite gentleman.

"Fancy meeting you here, Lane darling," she cooed, completely ignoring Paige.

"Hello, Jill," he replied, his voice as smooth as silk.

As much as Paige loathed to admit it, Jill Taylor was beautiful. She was small and dainty, with short brown hair that swirled against her creamy complexion every time she turned her head. With a pert, upturned nose and large brown eyes, she was exquisite. Her only flaw was that she leaned toward being plump, or maybe voluptuous was a better word, if one wasn't envious, that is.

The way she was making eyes at Lane made Paige want to punch in her pouting scarlet mouth. Still totally ignoring Paige's presence, she said, "If you're not busy tonight, I'm having a small get together at my apartment, I sure would like you to come."

Paige's chest felt as if it were going to cave in. She waited, holding her breath, for Lane's answer.

"Sorry, Jill, but I think not. My time isn't my own anymore." His eyes narrowed. "By the way, I don't think you've had the pleasure of meeting my wife." His gaze sought Paige's and their eyes locked and held.

"Very well, darling, I get the message for now. But remember when you get tired of your little wifey— again—I'll be waiting." Like a whirlwind she turned and marched back to her table and then out the door alone.

Paige stared at Lane, her eyes full of daggers. "How dare you let her get away with saying something like that?"

"Can't you see she only said what she did to cause trouble?" His mouth twisted. "Evidently she's going to get her wish."

Lane's calm logic had a soothing effect on her blazing anger. Swallowing hard, she said tonelessly, "It's just that I feel so…"

"Forget Jill," he interrupted. "We have plans to make."

Although Paige acquiesced, she was still seething inside. She realized she hadn't heard the last of Jill Taylor.

"Paige…" Lane gently prodded, "let's eat, shall we?"

She ate her lunch, but it had no taste.

"Tomorrow we'll get your clothes and whatever

else you want to keep and move them into my apartment.''

"Tomorrow…?''

"Yes, tomorrow, and the day after Christmas, we'll be flying to Belgium for a month. You'll need to make arrangements to be away from the store.''

Paige stared at him in disbelief. The walls of the room were closing in on her. Her time had run out—beginning tomorrow, she would once again be Mrs. Lane Morgan.

Seven

As the Boeing 747 flew toward London, Paige laid her head against the cushioned head rest and closed her eyes. After nearly three weeks of living as Mrs. Lane Morgan, she was now on her way to Antwerp, Belgium, via London.

She wished she could feel some enthusiasm for the trip that lay ahead of her. But the thought of being in Lane's pocket for nearly a month made her blood turn to ice water.

She was unsure of herself and even more unsure of Lane. Every time he came near her or touched her, her pulse raced, but at the same time she panicked. Although she had made up her mind to make the best of the situation, she still couldn't handle the thought of sharing Lane's bed.

Much to her chagrin she ached for his touch in that way. But the price was too big to pay for a few months of pleasure. She had to keep him away from her at night.

Even knowing she was to visit the diamond capital of the world did nothing to ensure any enthusiasm.

Paige raised her head slightly and peered at her husband out of the corner of her eye. He, too, was relaxing with his head back. The last two-and-a-half weeks had been thoroughly exhausting ones for them both. They had been working nonstop. As a result, she was exhausted.

The moment her belongings had been deposited in Lane's apartment, their lives had taken on the status of a roller coaster traveling at full speed. The highs were good, but the lows were miserably low. Her encounter with Ron concerning her month's leave of absence had been one of her lows. After an extended session of listening to his arguments, she had finally obtained his permission, but only after she had threatened to quit. Behind every word he had uttered, lay his absolute disapproval of her decision to go back to Lane. She shuddered to think what his reaction would have been had he known the truth.

The night before Lane had collected her paraphernalia, she had been a bundle of nerves. She had been positive that he would expect her to share his bedroom as well as his bed. But to her relief, he had had Joseph deposit her luggage in the smaller, but still spacious, second bedroom. Paige had felt her face flush a bright red at Lane's mocking, knowing look.

However, he had made no move to entice her to share any intimacies with him. In fact, at times, he had seemed almost indifferent toward her. Because they had been busy with Christmas, she hadn't let it prey on her mind.

In spite of the upheaval and change in her life, she had enjoyed the holiday. Lane had been charming. He had purchased lavish presents for Katherine and Jamie and had given Paige two specially designed diamond hair clips. They had had Christmas dinner with her family. For that day, all their hostilities had been cast aside.

Although Lane had made no demands on her physical body, she nevertheless was aware of his desire every minute she was with him. She saw it in his gaze as he followed her every move. Lurking, too, in the shadow of his eyes was that same sadness which he, at times, didn't bother to conceal. He seemed to be bent, in some grim fashion, on punishing himself as well as her.

If he were only resentful because they didn't occupy the same bedroom, she could possibly understand him. But *she* was the one with the sole right to be sad. After all, *she* was the one who nearly had died after she had lost their baby.

Her scars were deep and the tears of yesterday couldn't be erased easily. But Lane didn't even know that they had nearly been parents. He hadn't shed any tears.

A baby's cry from the rear of the compartment brought Paige swiftly back to the moment at hand. At times, that sound still had the power to lance her heart. She had wanted her baby so desperately. But it was not meant to be...

She began fidgeting in her seat to try and break the melancholy mood that had descended upon her. Knowing Lane was awake, since she could feel his eyes on her, she tried to avoid his gaze. He had an uncanny aptitude for being able to read her thoughts.

To prove she was as adept at hiding her thoughts as he was, she turned toward him. She was shocked at the emotion she saw displayed on his face. That strange sadness was back in his eyes and quickly she averted her gaze.

Surely the baby's cry hadn't anything to do with it? That's impossible she told herself. *It has to be something else.* Every so often, a twinge of guilt hit her when she wondered whether she should have told him.

A few minutes later, when she again ventured to look in his direction, his mood had lightened considerably. In fact, a grin was plastered on his face. "You can relax," he said, his tone husky. "I told you, I'm in no hurry to get you in my bed. I can wait..."

For a moment, Paige was torn between being both glad that he had misread the reason for her frustration, and angry at his audacity in thinking she was desperate to get into his bed. She refused to look him in the eye. "That's not it. I—" She gnawed at her lower lip.

"Shhh!" he said, leaning toward her, "Whatever it is, let's not worry about it right now."

Lane then proceeded to wipe the perturbed look off her face by laying his warm lips against hers. It was a fleetingly gentle kiss, but Paige felt her senses reel from its impact.

"Mmmm, you taste delicious, Mrs. Morgan. I'd like another taste. A man could get hooked on potent stuff like that."

Before Paige actually realized his intentions, his lips attached themselves to hers once again. This time, he was serious.

It was a long sweet kiss, his tongue thrusting deeply into her mouth, seeking the sweetness he knew was there. Without being conscious of it, Paige responded with an enthusiasm to match his. When he finally raised his head, she fought for her breath, too bemused to speak.

Paige could only nod when the flight attendant approached and asked for her if she cared for anything to drink.

With a twinkle in his eyes, Lane answered for her. "Bring her a Tom Collins and me a beer."

With a smile and a nod, the attendant made her way up the aisle to return shortly with their drinks.

There was silence between them as they each became lost in their own thoughts. Paige still tasted the soul-searching kiss she and Lane had shared a moment ago.

Breaking abruptly into her thoughts once more, Lane asked, "What do you say we call a halt to all hostilities and enjoy this trip? Let's play pretend?" He grinned.

Paige drew back and looked at him with raised eyebrows. "It depends on what you mean by 'let's pretend'." There was a measure of mistrust in her expression.

Lane laughed out loud. "Where's your sense of adventure, woman?"

"Huh!" she spat back at him, a smile playing at the corners of her mouth. "I trust you, Lane Morgan, about as far as I can throw you and *you* know how far that is."

"Well, how's this? If I promise not to do anything you don't want me to, will you go along with me and really make an effort to enjoy yourself?" Although his eyes were sparkling with mischief, his voice was serious.

Paige chewed her lower lip for a moment before replying softly, "All right, I'll try it your way."

"Good, you won't regret it, I promise."

"Well, I can't have you accusing me of having no sense of adventure, now can I?" she questioned saucily. A wide grin alighted her features and Lane found himself drowning in her beauty.

Paige, too, was affected by his look, but averted her head quickly. When Lane was in this kind of mood, she knew she had to keep her distance. He knew her too well, and she wasn't nearly a good enough liar.

"Oh, by the way," Lane said, too casually, "before I forget." He paused, leaning over and getting his billfold out of his back pocket. Opening it, he pulled out a credit card and laid it on Paige's lap. "While I'm at the 'sights' I want you to go to Harrod's and buy yourself a new wardrobe—the works."

Paige studied him for a moment then shook her head decisively. "No. I won't. I don't need the clothes, and it's not your place to…"

"Hush!" Lane interrupted. "As I remember correctly, we made an agreement. It seems to me you're not living up to your end."

She pouted prettily. "It escapes me how buying new clothes has anything to do with my sense of adventure."

He tipped his head back and laughed. "Oh, I don't know so much about that. It seems as if it all fits under the same category to me. Anyway I want you to have the clothes, especially to wear in Belgium."

His look was almost a husbandly request and Paige didn't have the heart to throw his generous offer back in his face. She did need some new clothes and it would be fun not to have to worry about their cost.

Paige smiled in agreement and hastily placed the card in her purse. She felt Lane draw a relaxed breath as he once again leaned back against the cushion.

Although she would now have her shopping expedition to look forward to during their short stay in London, she wished instead that she could accompany Lane to the "sights." However, she was not allowed.

Being invited by Central Selling Organization in London, a branch of DeBeers, to participate in their "sights" was an honor. Although she was familiar with DeBeers, as was everyone in the jewelry business, the big deals which were made and carried out in London remained an enigma to her.

Since she wouldn't be able to accompany Lane, there were several questions she was eager to ask him. There had virtually been no time to pin him down. Now was her chance, since he was in a relatively good and relaxed mood.

"Lane?" she questioned tentatively.

He turned toward her and smiled, waiting.

She hesitated. "My curiosity has gotten the better of me. Would you mind telling me what is involved when you are invited to participate in the 'sights'?"

Lane's face lighted up with pleasure. "As you already know, it's an honor just to be invited. I'm one of about two hundred buyers who have earned the privilege to buy in advance from DeBeers. We are chosen for our financial strength and, more importantly, for our dependability."

"In other words," chimed in Paige, "you've now reached the pinnacle of success in your business."

Denoting no sarcasm in her tone, Lane smiled. "Let me put it this way. I'm proud of what I've accomplished in such a short time, but there's still a lot more room for improvement. I plan to move on—to be satisfied with your lot in life is merely to stagnate. Agree?"

"Sounds right to me," Paige said cautiously. She wasn't sure exactly what point he was trying to make, so she agreed and asked him another question. "Exactly what happens when all two hundred jewelers get together? Who gets what diamonds?"

Lane smiled. "Would you believe we actually have no choice in the matter?"

Paige shook her head. "I had read where this was true, but it's honestly hard for me to comprehend."

"Well, you'd best believe it, because it's true. I will be allotted a small cloth bag. In that bag will be rough diamonds of different categories and sizes." He paused, taking a drink of his beer. "While you're out shopping I'll be studying the stones in my parcel."

"What if you're not pleased with them?"

He shrugged. "It's too bad. Take all or nothing, and immediate cash."

"You'd better hope you don't get duped," Paige uttered, blinking her large blue eyes.

He grimaced. "It's not something I even like to think about. However, it's rare for a client to be really unhappy with his lot. I've heard of only a few instances where that's happened. Of course, I'm sure there'll be a few bad stones mixed with the good ones."

She frowned. "Will we be taking them to Antwerp with us?" She wasn't too excited about that possibility. Just the thought of it spelled danger.

Lane rolled his eyes upwards. "Good heavens, no. I'll have them go out by registered mail direct to my factory in Antwerp." He grinned. "No muss, no fuss."

Paige smiled, her face relaxing a little, "Then I'll be able to see them cut and polished while we're there. Right?"

"Right. Barring complications that is."

"I'm sure everything will go exactly as planned," she said, her face lit with a smile.

His only comment was to let his gaze wander over her face, coming to rest on her lips. Refusing to meet his eyes, she averted her head and made a pretence of looking out the window of the plane. *I must remain aloof,* she reminded herself once again.

The remainder of the flight was uneventful. Paige drifted into a rather deep sleep and was awakened by Lane when they landed at Heathrow Airport in London.

Jet lag had left its mark on her. She barely remembered the taxi ride from the airport to the Hilton Hotel in downtown London where Lane had booked them into separate rooms. They went to bed immediately and didn't get up until noon the next day.

Time passed very quickly for Paige while they were in London. They stayed only three days, and while Lane took care of his business, she occupied herself, enjoying every minute to the fullest.

She shopped, trying on clothes to her heart's content. She bought clothes which she thought she might wear in Belgium, purchasing mix-and-match separates, crush resistant blouses and dresses and two different styles of raincoats. Lane had told her that it rained often in Antwerp and whatever she purchased, she shouldn't forget rain apparel. She also chose several comfortable pairs of walking shoes as well as dinner dresses and evening wear. And daringly, she treated herself to a small designer bottle of Oscar de la Renta perfume.

She went to an exclusive beauty salon and had her hair shaped and styled into soft waves that framed her face. She visited Buckingham Palace and had lunch in several famous London restaurants. When she became tired, she went to her hotel room, rested and began all over again.

Although they adjourned to their separate rooms each night, Paige never felt completely comfortable when she was in Lane's presence. When he touched her, whether by accident or on purpose, her spine tingled. The uneasy truce between them was liable to erupt at any time and almost did during their last night in London.

They had gone out to dinner. Throughout the meal Lane had seemed moody, preoccupied and there was very little conversation between them. He had insisted on walking her to her room, which was unusual, since in the past they had parted at the elevator.

She had turned her questioning eyes up to him to whisper good night. For a moment, they had become lost in each other. To Paige, it seemed as if their souls touched. Lane was the first to draw away.

"Paige...I..."

She felt as if the breath had been knocked out of her. She couldn't move.

"Oh, hell," he muttered rubbing his neck in weary agitation. "Never mind." He then turned on his heel and strode to his room.

It was early morning before she closed her eyes.

Finally, Lane finished his business in London. After three fun-filled days and nights, Paige found herself beside her husband on a plane bound for Belgium.

She could hardly contain her excitement as the small jet airliner made its way the short distance from London's Heathrow Airport to Antwerp. Paige was barely settled before the "fasten seat belts" light flashed on above her. She began scrambling around for the seat belt, trying to get situated so she wouldn't miss any of the scenery. She heard a guttural chuckle as Lane brushed her hands away, proceeding to latch the belt for her.

Warm color invaded her cheeks as his gaze flickered

over her face. His eyes moved slowly over her cheek-bones, her nose, her moisture ridden mouth, then upward to her eyes. She melted under his burning gaze.

It didn't take Lane long to move through the hassle of customs in Antwerp. Before she had a chance to even see the airport, she found herself in a taxi bound for the Plaza Hotel.

Their driver, turning to them in the back seat, said with a grin on his face, "Welcome to Antwerp." Then, pausing, he raised his eyes skyward. "And be thankful it's not raining!"

Paige grinned. She loved his accent and wanted him to continue talking, but he turned his attention back to his driving.

"Well, what do you think?" Lane asked as he peered at her out of half-closed eyes. "Are you prepared to enjoy yourself?"

"Oh, yes," she exclaimed enthusiastically, her eyes sparkling.

"Even with the rain, it's a fun country to visit. My business dealings at the factory will be limited, so I'll have plenty of time to show you the sights."

The trip from the airport was short, and Paige saw very little of the countryside except to note how green and flat it was. So early the next morning, Lane knocked on the door of her room to wake her up. He had rented a car, and planned to take her on a tour of the outskirts of Antwerp as well as the city itself.

Although it had been raining during the early morning, the temperature, for December, was rather mild, only in the fifties. She wore straight-legged khaki pants with a bulky sweater and a pair of comfortable lace-up shoes. She pinned her hair up on top of her head, donning her rain hat and matching coat and remembered, just in time, to grab her umbrella.

Since Lane had been to Antwerp many times, he was the perfect guide. They stopped by his diamond cutting factory on the outskirts of Antwerp for a few minutes and Paige got her first look at the workings of the diamond industry on a large scale.

The only way Lane got her to leave was to promise to let her see the whole operation several times before returning to the States. He assured her when the rough stones came in from London, she would be able to see them put through the finishing process from beginning to end. She had to be content with his promise for the moment.

On their trek through the countryside, she found the people extremely friendly and the streets and countryside immaculately clean. No matter where they drove, each person they passed gave them a big smile and waved. Flowers lined the lush green meadows and front yards everywhere they traveled.

During the late afternoon, Lane made a quick tour of downtown Antwerp with a special emphasis on the Kennedy Tunnel which linked old Antwerp with the new Antwerp. Paige was fascinated with the huge tunnel and with the stands on every street corner, selling everything from coffee, to crème cakes, to fried potatoes. After some persuasion, Paige managed to get

Lane to stop in front of the nearest stand, at which golden potatoes were being dished out briskly.

With an indulgent smile on his face, Lane said, "You know I don't mind you having them, but it's so late, I'd hate for you to ruin your appetite. I have a really special dinner planned."

Paige wrinkled her nose as she pondered his words. "Well," she said, shrugging her shoulders, "maybe you're right." She laughed. "I'll save the fries, the crème cakes and the chocolates all for tomorrow!"

Lane laughed aloud. "Woman," he challenged, "I didn't bring you all this way just to get you fat. How will I ever be able to justify an overindulged wife to my friends?" His eyes twinkled as he looked at her with what he hoped was a serious face.

"Huh!" she retaliated, casting slanted eyes at him. "I was under the impression your taste had changed and you liked your women a little, un—," she paused, as if searching for the right words, "a little overweight."

His face hardened at the reminder of Jill, and his eyes grew accusing. "One of these days, Paige, you're going to back yourself into a corner you can't get out of."

She resented his manner, and snapped back, "I already have. I did the minute I agreed to go back to you in order to bail Jamie out of trouble."

The anger showed on his face as he turned away from her. His hands gripped the steering wheel so tightly that they whitened.

What in the world made her say such a thing to

him? They were having such a good time. For once, there was no undercurrent between them. He was behaving like the Lane she had married.

She had panicked. Maybe that was why she said it—to break the enchanted spell. She kept forgetting to remind herself that they had no future.

Lane remained an extremely polite but formal companion throughout the rest of the day and evening. He took her to what he termed one of the best restaurants in Antwerp, The Criterium, where they ordered the house speciality, duckling and the country's famed Brussels sprouts, cooked to perfection in pork drippings. With their dinner, they drank the house wine.

However, as far as Paige was concerned, she might as well have been eating paper. It was times like this when she questioned her good sense. She was a fool and she knew it.

In fact, she despised herself. A look, a touch, a smile and her insides ran like molten lava. How would she be able to remain in his company for the next few weeks and not do something she would regret for the rest of her life?

However, the next morning Lane's good humor was somewhat restored. The day began as the previous one had, with his waking her up early with their day's activities planned. As usual, it was raining, so Paige again dressed comfortably in slacks, sweater and raincoat. The first stop on the agenda was a street stand in downtown Antwerp for a hot pastry and a cup of coffee.

Having fortified themselves, Lane became nothing

short of a tour guide, showing her many of the most famous places and sights of the city. They visited the Royal Museum of Fine Arts and viewed what seemed like a thousand Flemish and Dutch masterpieces. From there they went to the zoological gardens, which housed over six thousand animals.

After stopping at a street cafe and dining on a link of boudin sausage, they spent the afternoon in Middleheim Park. Paige was completely in awe of the over two hundred modern sculptures that were on open-air display.

By the time Lane pulled the Porsche to a halt in front of the hotel, Paige was exhausted. The doorman helped her out, and when Lane came around the car to join her, she flashed him a tired smile.

"I don't know about you, but I'm beat." She pulled her rain hat off her head and ran her hands through her thick mahogany hair.

"Same here," he replied, leaning over to brush a strand of hair out of her eyes, his hand lingering as he stationed the wayward lock behind her ear.

She looked up at him and was captured by the haunting darkness of his eyes. She stifled the impulse to reach up and stroke his cheek. Her heart hammered. But the moment passed as the elevator announced its arrival with its clanging bell and red light. Taking a deep breath, Paige hastily joined the other occupants, standing as far away from Lane as possible.

She fumed inwardly. Even though he hadn't made an effort to get her into his bed, his daring seemed to increase every day. He took every chance available to touch her in some way. A hand accidently nudging her breast, causing the nipple to harden immediately within the confines of her bra, a helping hand across the street and, last but not least, the ever present arm, resting across her shoulders as they wandered aimlessly through the museum and the zoo.

To make matters worse, she could have stopped him, but hadn't. What had happened to her resolve to keep her perspective, to be cool? She couldn't blame anyone except herself for her predicament.

There was a heavy silence between them as they got off the elevator and walked down the carpeted hallway to their adjoining rooms.

Paige felt Lane's eyes on her. "Are a couple of hours long enough for you to rest before dinner?"

Keeping her face averted, Paige began, "I really don't think I'm up to..."

He swung her around to face him. "Don't go all cold on me now, Paige," he said, his voice tense. "One minute you're running hot, the next minute you freeze up like a block of ice." He expelled a harsh sigh. "How in hell am I supposed to keep up with your moods?"

"You're not!" she retorted waspishly.

His mouth thinned. "Paige, I'm warning you," he ground out through clenched teeth, "don't push me too far..."

"Don't you push *me* too far!" she flung back at him, eyes flashing. She then swung her head around making sure no one else was in the hall to hear their heated exchange.

Lane's shoulders sagged. "Maybe you're right, we need some breathing room." His whole attitude expressed utter frustration.

With a soft caress of his finger against her cheek, he said, "Rest well, my dear. I'll see you in the morning." With that, he turned and walked away.

Paige found herself alone. She skipped dinner and cried herself to sleep.

The next morning she woke up with dried tears on her face. Her eyes were puffy and swollen. She gave a loud moan after making her way to the adjoining bath and staring at herself in the mirror.

As she showered, she wondered if she would hear from Lane or if he would leave her to her own devices. She sighed aloud as she dried her long shapely limbs with a bath towel. *Maybe Lane is right to give us breathing room,* she thought.

It took twice the amount of makeup she usually wore to cover the dark circles and blotched places on her face. After putting on an emerald green soft wool dress, she surveyed her image once more in the mirror and, to her surprise, was pleased with her appearance.

Paige was in the process of pushing a pair of diamond stud earrings in her ears, when a soft rap on the door caused her to pause.

She hesitated. "Lane? Is that you?"

"Yes," he announced quietly.

"Come on in. The door's open," she returned, uneasiness lacing her voice.

As he opened the door and crossed the threshold, his cologne drifted through the room, making her aware more than ever of his strong attraction. She let none of her feelings show, however, as she gave him a tentative smile.

Cocking his head to one side, he looked deeply into her blue eyes. "The stones from London arrived early this morning. Would you like to visit the factory today and watch the cutting process?"

Her eyes brightened. "Would I!" she exclaimed. "You knew I would without even asking. Can we go now?"

Paige was unaware of the picture she presented to Lane as she stood before him, the green in her dress enhancing the richness of her hair and her delicate complexion.

He averted his gaze and in a brusque tone said, "I'm ready. Where's your raincoat?" His eyes searched the room until they found her rain gear draped across a chair in the corner. He turned suddenly and moved to get it.

The day passed too quickly for Paige. Upon arriving at the factory, Lane immediately introduced her to his top diamond cutter, Mr. Perevian. He was a short, stout man with a ready smile, whom she liked on sight.

Without any preliminaries, Mr. Perevian placed a large rough looking stone on his work table and proceeded to explain to Paige what he was about to do. Paige hovered close, with Lane stationed not far from her, an indulgent smile on his face as he took in her enthusiasm.

The little man pointed to the stone in front of him

and said to her in his heavy accent. "As you probably already know, the beauty and brilliance of this stone comes from within. What I'm about to do is to release that brilliance."

Paige nodded, enraptured.

"However," he continued, "the less work that is done, the better, because each step has its dangers. It will be a slow process as I don't want to end up with a lot of broken glass." He chuckled, knowing full well he was a master at his craft.

"I'm following you so far," Paige replied, her eyes still glued to his hands.

"Good," he acknowledged. "Now watch carefully…"

For the next few hours, Paige sat without moving, watching every step he made. He first detected the direction of the grain, marking the outlines carefully with India ink. Having duly inked the stone, he took the first crucial step in cleaving it. With a knife-shaped diamond chip, he cut a V-shaped groove in the top of the stone, in line with the grain assessment. He then inserted a blunt-edged wedge and gently tapped it with a special mallet.

Paige expelled a sigh of relief as the diamond split neatly apart, dividing the grain perfectly.

The next step was the cutting process which involved placing the diamond in a small metal cup. The cup was mounted on a machine next to another diamond, which was the only substance that would cut it.

As the stone spun, Mr. Perevian pressed the other

diamond to it at right angles. The friction between the two diamonds chipped off the rough spots and corners. Gradually Paige saw the outline of a pear-shaped stone emerge. Mr. Perevian then took the stone, grinding it and polishing it until it shone with the required number of facets and faces.

She was tired but still sparkling from her day at the factory when Lane saw her to her door later that evening. They had stopped for dinner at a quiet cafe and, along with a bottle of wine, had eaten one of the Belgian specialities, baby eels served cold. To her amazement, she thought it was delicious.

Harmony existed between them once again, although they both obviously kept from touching each other. The strain of being together constantly was leaving its mark on Paige.

The next three weeks did nothing to alleviate the tension. Although Lane tended to a vast amount of business at his factory, he insisted that Paige accompany him. She kept her sketch pad out and her pencil busy. Seeing so many beautifully cut stones, her mind buzzed with ideas for stunning pieces of jewelry.

Paige was completely in awe of and proud of what Lane had accomplished. As soon as his cutters completed their work, the designers and craftsmen took over, and beautiful pieces of jewelry were created and shipped to all of Lane's stores throughout the United States.

She longed, at times, to hurry and get back home so she could go to work with her designs. Then she would remember Ron and his predicament. Her enthusiasm waned.

When Paige and Lane weren't at his factory, they took in more of the sights of Antwerp and Brussels. They spent time touring several of the well known caves and toured the port for which Antwerp was famous. They spent time at the Provincial Diamond Museum. They paraded through the open-air antique market, the street markets, where she ate Belgian chocolates until she was nearly sick, and the common market, where Lane purchased fine linen and lace shawls for both her and her mother. Paige's favorite place was the glass-roofed Galerie St. Hubert, a shopper's paradise. There were excellent buys on leather goods, which Lane couldn't pass up for himself and Jamie.

Throughout the time spent exclusively in Lane's company, he made it a point not to touch her. Because he made such a point of not doing so, it was all the more obvious. She could see the desire, mixed with sadness and at times brooding anger, in his eyes. She was at a loss as to how to combat the emotions his glances evoked within her. She tried not to think about him in that way.

The bright sunlight streaming through the filtered draperies drew Paige out of her deep sleep. She wanted to roll over and go back to sleep, but she remembered that this was her last day in Belgium.

She bounced out of bed, thrilled with the chilly but sunny day. Lane had planned a cycling trip for them through the countryside. The weather couldn't have been more perfect.

Glancing at her watch, she noticed she only had thirty minutes before she was to meet Lane downstairs. She quickly showered, applied her makeup and put on a pair of jeans and a heavy sweater, not letting herself be fooled by the bright sunlight.

They both ate hearty breakfasts. Laughing like two children they rented bicycles from the hotel and sped on their way.

As they pedaled side by side down an uncrowded lane, Paige glanced sideways at her husband. He was attired the same as she, in blue jeans and a heavy sweater. His freshly shaven face glowed in the beauty of the morning and the lines around the corner of his mouth seemed less strained.

Feeling her gaze on him, he turned. Their eyes met and held for a timeless moment.

Words locked in her throat. *I want him,* she thought with blinding honesty. *I want Lane Morgan, my husband.*

His eyes narrowed gently. ''A penny for your thoughts.''

She swallowed with difficulty. ''I'm afraid they're not even worth half a penny.'' Her voice was husky as she averted her gaze.

His eyes caressed her. ''Oh, I don't know,'' he drawled lazily. ''Why don't you let me be the judge of that?''

She shook her head, causing the loose knot of hair at the nape of her neck to come undone. It flowed freely about her shoulders and began blowing in the wind. "Oh, drat!" she hissed, as she tried to push the silken locks out of her face. She was near tears. He was so close she could touch him, and yet he was miles away.

Lane laughed. "Don't get your dander up, honey. Pull over to the side and we'll fix it."

Before Paige had a chance to scrounge around for something to secure it with, she felt the smooth touch of Lane's fingers against her skin as he slowly drew the thick mass of hair back, tying it with a piece of gauze taken from the first-aid kit he carried in the satchel on his bicycle. She felt his breath filter across her naked skin, causing a chill to cascade up and down her spine. She began to fidget nervously.

"Be still, woman," Lane demanded, chuckling. "How do you expect me to do anything with you squirming this way and that."

When Lane finally completed his task, she turned and flashed him a quick, grateful smile. They set out once again, pedaling at full speed.

Paige's thoughts, the further they rode, became clouded. As she gazed about her, she was sad to say goodbye to this charming country. By this time the following morning, they would be on their way back to Texas.

She dreaded what lay ahead of her; Ron and his problem and her bargain with Lane, Jamie's trial and last but not least her questionable relationship with her husband.

"What's the matter with you this morning?" Lane

asked, breaking into her thoughts. "Aren't you having a good time?"

"Of course, I'm having a good time—it's just that—"

"Well, come on then," he interrupted, "get the lead out of your feet and I'll race you across the bridge."

She threw him a quick smile. "You're on! Let's go."

Of course, Lane reached the other side of the bridge long before she did. He waited for her with a triumphant smile alighting his features.

Seeing him standing against his bicycle with a smug look on his face made Paige do what she would shortly come to regret. She aimed the nose of her cycle straight for Lane with the intention of swerving at the last minute so as to just miss him.

But as she hurled toward him and started to turn, the gears on her bicycle locked, and she couldn't turn or stop.

Lane sidestepped out of the way just in time, and yelled, "For God's sake, Paige, jump!" In front of her was a deep pool of water surrounded by a lush green meadow.

Her eyes widened as she took him at his word.

The last thing she remembered was rolling down the hill with a frightened Lane running behind her.

The sun slid behind a black cloud...

She awoke hours later with a sense of panic, completely disoriented. Then she remembered her fall and groaned as she placed her hand on the bump on the back of her head. Surprisingly, though, it wasn't unduly painful.

The door slowly opened, and a harassed looking Lane crossed the threshold. The muted glow from the lamplight played havoc with his features. He looked dreadful. And there was a frightened look on his face. Her eyes widened as he made his way to the foot of the bed.

With suppressed emotion, he rasped, "I could kill you for what you did to me today."

Eight

Paige struggled to sit up in the bed, but her body wouldn't comply. Her limbs felt like jelly. "I'm sorry," she gasped as she fell back against the pillow.

Lane was around the bed in a second. "Sorry!" he exploded. "Is that all you have to say after nearly killing yourself?" He paused, sucking in his breath and then expelling it slowly. "I almost lost my mind until the doctor examined you and assured me you were in no real danger."

"I'm—I'm sorry," she gulped, tears blinding her vision. His image swam before her eyes. She turned her head sideways into the pillow.

She felt his weight as he eased himself down beside her on the bed. His warm breath danced across her face as he leaned over and gently turned her head around to confront him.

They looked at each other for a long moment. The tears shimmered in her eyes. Neither one spoke. His eyes roamed over her with slow deliberation. She felt a jolt of electricity course through her body at his look of smoldering desire.

Lane drew a deep relieved breath. "Are you hungry?" he asked softly. "How does a bowl of hot vegetable soup sound?'' His eyes still devoured her, as he took in the beguiling picture she made with her hair fanned in disarray against the pillow. The creamy smoothness of her shoulders was tantalizing him almost to distraction.

She gave him a semblance of a smile. ''Believe it or not, I'm starving.'' She paused to wipe a lone tear off her cheek. ''In fact,'' she grinned shyly, ''I feel good, considering what happened to me, that is.''

His eyes darkened. ''Thank God,'' he stated forcefully. ''The doctor told me you shouldn't have too many ill effects—maybe a headache. But I didn't completely trust him…''

''What happened after I…uh…blacked out?'' she asked hesitantly, the tip of her tongue moistening her lips. The round softness of her eyes stared at him in trepidation.

Lane sighed deeply as he rubbed the back of his neck. ''If it hadn't been for the deep soft grass, every bone in your body might have been broken.'' He shuddered. ''There was a farm house nearby, and the old man who lived there called the local doctor. He checked you over the best he could and drove us back to the hotel. Don't you remember?'' His voice was full of concern.

''Not much, to be honest,'' she responded helplessly. ''I'm lucky the wallop I received on the back of my head didn't cause a concussion, aren't I?''

''You sure as hell are! What in the world made you do a stupid thing like that anyway?''

"I was only trying to teach you a lesson," she said defensively.

"You taught me a lesson all right," he declared brusquely. "One I won't ever forget, either."

She looked puzzled. "I know it was stupid, but I didn't mean to cause so much tro—"

"Shhh!" he interrupted, touching her lips lightly with his fingers. "It's over and done with. Just remind me not to ever challenge you to another race." He grinned, his eyes drawn once again to her creamy shoulders. The strap of her bra draped lazily downward, beguiling him like a satin bow on a package he didn't dare open.

Paige trembled.

Smiling, he got up from the bed. "Is there anything you need me to do for you before I go get you something to eat?"

"No." Her tongue clung to the dry roof of her mouth. "I think I'll take a quick shower while you're gone."

"Well, be careful," he told her huskily.

It dawned on her when she got in the bathroom that she only had on her bra and panties. She felt herself grow red thinking about Lane's hands on her body and the deep, veiled looks he gave her just now in the bedroom.

After taking a slow easy shower, she powdered herself with a fresh smelling scent and brushed her hair vigorously. She donned a pale yellow nightgown, and had just returned to the bed when Lane rapped on the door and entered with a tray in his hands.

"Are you all right?" he asked smiling.

She smiled in return. "I feel like a new woman."

"Well, I guarantee what I have here will make you feel even better. I want to see you devour every last drop," he told her smoothly as he placed the tray unceremoniously on her lap.

There was very little conversation between them as she devoured every morsel of the soup, hot buttered bread and cheesecake he brought her.

After removing the tray, Lane walked to the window and stared out at the city while he waited for her to return from the bathroom. His shoulders slumped wearily. *How I hate to leave her,* he thought to himself. His gut feeling told him he was about to make a fool of himself for a second time.

Paige, returning from brushing her teeth, missed him when she stepped back into the muted glow of the room.

"Lane?" she questioned softly, uncertainty hovering on the edge of her voice.

He turned around and faced her from across the room.

Paige's bones turned to water under his scrutiny. His eyes stroked her, inflaming her senses. When she bent to hide her face, her hair fell with unconscious sensuality about her shoulders.

She heard the sharp intake of his breath as he made his way toward her. He stopped short of touching her—waiting, questioning until she looked up at him with trust in her eyes.

A sweet smile tugged at the corners of his mouth

as he raised his fingers and reached to touch her lips. Leisurely he traced their outline until she managed to trap his finger between her teeth and caress the tip of it with her tongue.

She heard his moan as he removed his finger and pulled her up against his long hard frame. Still he didn't kiss her. He gently pressed her head against his shoulder and folded her more tightly against him, holding her.

Paige sighed, snuggling deeper.

Sensing her willingness, Lane brushed aside the hair at the nape of her neck and began planting soft moist kisses on her skin.

She was aware of his body—the passion building within him. The scent of his flesh and his hair was his alone, the combination of clean and fresh.

After a moment of holding her, he grudgingly loosened his grip and pushed her back so that they were face to face once again. "Paige," he rasped. "Are you sure?"

"Yes," she breathed, her voice barely audible in the quiet room.

No other words were necessary.

Lane leaned closer and covered her mouth with his own, delivering a gentle, lingering kiss. She bound him closer to her with her arms, meeting his mouth, hungrily, like a starving child. His tongue sparred with hers. He groaned under the onslaught of their engulfing pleasure.

Unlocking his arms, he picked her up and carried her the short distance to the bed. Paige felt the mattress give under their weight as he laid her down gently and lowered himself beside her. He looked at her briefly before leaning over and placing hot, nibbling kisses across the top of each breast exposed to his covetous eyes.

His kisses sent darting spasms of response throughout her body. Then he lowered his lips to enclose a nipple, nurturing and tugging at it through the confines of her gown. At her gasp of pleasure, Lane once more worked his way up to her mouth. As their lips and tongues collided, the liquid fire raged from within.

Paige gave as she took. Nibbling and tonguing his ear, she matched his love play stroke for stroke.

Needing and wanting more, Lane lay down beside her. He placed his hand in the small of her back and aligned her small frame next to his. She moved to get closer, causing the heat to build up in Lane almost to the boiling point. A guttural sound erupted from his throat as he rolled over, pinning her beneath him.

"Lane, oh, Lane," she sighed as she traced the outline of his jaw with her fingers, mesmerized by the burning passion she saw in his eyes.

Shyly Paige ran her hand under Lane's sweater, raising it upward. Amusement darkened his eyes as he took the hint and positioned himself on the side of the bed and quickly pulled the sweater over his head.

The wide expanse of his chest was open to her gaze. Her eyes never wandered as he moved to unfasten the snap at his waist. When his jeans had joined his sweater, he lowered himself beside her once again.

She placed her mouth on his collarbone, the side of

his neck, and the base of his throat and lower to the hardened bud encased in his hairy chest.

"Oh, God, Paige," he cried out in delight, "I can't take much more." He ran his hands downward across her hips, reaching for the end of her gown. He found it, and in one movement yanked it up and over her head, throwing it to the floor.

Their bodies were joined with nothing between them. Lane immediately fastened his lips around a breast and teased it with his tongue. It rose to a hard knot as he tormented it and then he moved to the other and did likewise.

"You're more beautiful than I remembered," he rasped, taking in the perfection of her limbs exposed to his ardent gaze under the lamplight.

Paige couldn't say a word. Her throat was swollen with desire.

His hands began a loving assault on her body. They moved from massaging her breast into full bloom, downward to her naval, and further. Paige had forgotten that one man could bring so much pleasure. She basked in the enjoyment his hands were bringing her. His mouth then followed the movement of his hands bringing her to further heights of rapture.

Sweetly he worshipped her.

When he reached the point of no return, his fingers slid down her thighs, opening her legs, gently positioning himself above her. He was there, easing forward. She lifted her arms bringing his head down to her breast, calling his name as he filled her completely.

Her hips shifted, perfectly timed to his slow movement. He touched a chord deep within her and her heart nearly exploded as the sweet pain of fusion completely and totally enveloped them.

They remained entwined, after having spent themselves into total exhaustion.

I still love him was the last thought that crossed her mind before she fell into a deep dreamless sleep.

Paige sat staring out of the plane's tiny window during the trip home to Houston. A tear escaped to gently slide down her cheek. She hastily brushed it aside, breathing deeply. She must make an effort to get hold of herself.

She could hardly fathom it. Nothing had changed. It was devastating enough to suddenly realize she still loved Lane, but for him to act as if *nothing* out of the ordinary had happened between them the night before was a defeating blow.

When she had awakened earlier that morning, the only evidence that Lane had shared her bed was the destructive condition of it. Their night of love making had had rare moments of tenderness, but for the most part, it had been more of the sweet-savage variety. She blushed, thinking about the way she had given herself to him in total abandonment with no thought of tomorrow.

It was with mixed emotions that she had left her room to meet Lane downstairs for breakfast.

What type of reaction could she expect from him?

He had been waiting for her at the entrance to the coffee shop. Seeing him standing there, dressed in a dark blue suit, looking big, handsome, endearing, made her insides quiver. With lips parted in eager anticipation, she had all but rushed up to him, and gently laid her hand on his arm.

He turned swiftly at her touch and for a moment she saw a spark of an unidentifiable emotion flare into his eyes. But all too soon, the shutter fell across his face. She was unable to read his expression. He said blandly, "You're late. I've booked us on an earlier flight, so we haven't much time to get packed and get to the airport."

Paige responded lightly. "Do we have to be in such a hurry?" She looked at him deeply and smiled. "After all, we're both tired..." Her voice held a huskiness which she couldn't quite conceal.

"Yes," he told her smiling, but not responding to her innuendo, "we do. There's a problem in Houston requiring my immediate attention." He pointedly glanced down at his watch, hidden amidst the dark hairs on his wrist. "Are you hungry?"

"No!" she tossed back, puzzled. "I wouldn't want to interfere with your schedule, not for one minute!" She threw back her head without attempting to hide her annoyance, and headed for the elevator.

"Paige, wait. I didn't mean—"

"Forget it," she replied coolly. "I'm just as ready to go now as you are."

He looked at her for a long tense moment, his expression unreadable.

She held her breath.

In an exasperated tone, he finally said, "I'll send the porter shortly to pick up your luggage."

A sob rose in her throat as she turned away and pushed the elevator button. She could feel his eyes boring into her back and prayed for the elevator to hurry. With shoulders straight she waited, refusing to let Lane see how much he had hurt her by his attitude. How naive she had been to imagine that what they had shared meant anything special to him.

By the time she reached her room she was shaking. *How could I love him?* she asked herself over and over as she paced the floor wasting precious time. But she had to admit that despite what had just taken place between them, she would never stop loving him.

The trip from the hotel to the airport had been made in strained silence. She had schooled her features to conceal her inner turmoil.

Now, as she studied the turbulent clouds drifting by the plane's window, she wondered whether she could manage to keep her renewed love a closely guarded secret. *I must,* she stressed to herself adamantly. But she found it hard to accept the fact that she had been only a one-night stand to Lane. With these disturbing thoughts, Paige forced herself to close her eyes and try to sleep.

Lane's firm but gentle shake on her shoulder awakened her immediately. Her eyes flew open and for a moment she felt her guard slip as she met his gaze. He raised his hand as if to touch her and then dropped it flatly. She could have sworn she saw a flicker of pain cross his eyes, but brushed the thought aside immediately as a figment of her imagination.

Paige turned away abruptly, reaching down to pick up her purse. Hot tears blurred her vision. She continued to fumble with her purse, keeping her hands busy until Lane rose and began retrieving his briefcase from the enclosed hamper above their seats.

They were greeted by a cold, rainy, dreary Houston. As Lane carefully maneuvered his car out of the airport parking lot, Paige shivered. Lane glanced at her briefly before saying, "There's an afghan in the back seat. Do you want it to throw over your legs until the car gets warm?"

"No, no," she managed to eke out between chattering teeth. "I'll—I'll be, be fine in a min-minute."

His only comment was to reach forward and flip the blower switch to high-maximum.

Paige was still tired but found it did no good to try and shut her eyes. Her thoughts were in chaos. She would be returning to work soon, which would help some. But that, too, was an albatross around her neck. Not because of work—she actually looked forward to that—it was the problem with Ron which she dreaded so much. And she wasn't looking forward to Jamie's trial either.

"Paige."

At the sound of her name, she pushed her thoughts aside and turned to face her husband.

"Yes?" she asked, her tone formal. She was amazed that she could be cool on the outside when inside she was in turmoil.

If he noticed her cold, standoffish tone, he chose to ignore it. "Would you have any objections to living in The Woodlands?"

Paige was completely taken by surprise at his question. She floundered momentarily for an answer. Gritting her teeth, she reminded herself that she was playing a game.

"Sounds fine to me," she replied smoothly.

"Well," he sighed, "I didn't really have a chance to discuss it with you before we left for Belgium, but I've been looking at houses there, thinking it would be a good place for Jamie to live."

She stared, lifting her delicate brows, "Do you mean you'd move mother and Jamie there, too?"

"That's what I had in mind," he declared lightly, "unless you object?" His eyes were questioning as they briefly flickered over her.

"No, no," she said haltingly, "not really." She shrugged her shoulders lightly. "You caught me by surprise that's all."

He looked at her closely in the dim light of the car. "Since you won't be working except one or two days a week, I thought you might enjoy living away from the city and having a large yard to putter around in, to say nothing of the trees you always said you wanted..."

His voice trailed off at the look of utter amazement that crossed her face. "What's the matter?" he questioned hesitantly. "Did I say something wrong?" His whole attitude was one of feigned innocence.

Paige averted her head. Here he was acting as if

they were the perfect married couple with a perfect marriage. He obviously didn't want her, since he couldn't even bear to discuss last night or to look her in the eyes since it happened. Yet, now he was behaving as if they were planning for a lifetime of marital bliss.

She sat like a carved wooden figure and said flatly, "No, you didn't say or do anything wrong, Lane— absolutely nothing, nothing at all."

She knew she had made her point. The rugged intake of his breath vibrated throughout the car's interior.

"Well," he muttered grimly, "you're right. I've skirted around the real issue long enough, haven't I? We've got to talk."

"Not now," she said, swallowing hard. "It's too late." She kept her eyes focused intently on her hands in her lap.

"Paige!" His voice was tormented. "Listen to me."

She shook her head firmly. "What is there to talk about now?" she asked in a frozen voice.

Lane uttered a muffled curse. "You know damn well what we have to talk about!" He swung expertly around the curve in the freeway. "Last night!"

Paige heaved a sigh. "Please, I-I'd rather not—not now…"

"I know what an unfeeling swine you think I am," he interrupted her savagely, "and believe me, I'm not proud of what happened or of myself!" He removed a hand from the steering wheel and rubbed his neck wearily.

Paige's breath caught in her throat. "For God's sake, Lane! Stop making a federal case out of it!"

"You just don't understand." A violent flame burned in his voice. "For me it is a federal case." He gnawed at his lower lip. "I swore I'd never let myself go that far…. Oh, hell…!"

She dug her fingernails into her hot palms. "Please!" she pleaded, "just forget it!"

His eyes narrowed. "Tell me, how can you be so damned indifferent about the whole thing?"

She felt her stomach churn and closed her eyes, completely ignoring him. *How much simpler and easier my life would be,* she thought to herself, *if I were indifferent.*

There was silence in the car the rest of the way home.

Joseph greeted them when they arrived at Lane's apartment and wanted to know if they wanted anything to eat.

"Nothing for me, Joseph," Lane said with a brief smile. "I'm going to the office."

Paige's face paled. More than likely, he was simply looking for an excuse to get away from her.

"How about you, Mrs. Morgan?" Joseph asked tentatively.

She frowned absently. "I—ah—I'll skip dinner tonight." Her eyes followed Lane's every movement. "I'm not really very hungry," she ended in a near whisper.

Lane eyed her intently from across the room. "You look tired."

"I am," she responded with a dejected sigh.

Lane hunched his shoulders. "I'll see you in the morning, then."

Looking at him for a moment longer, Paige suddenly thought he appeared lonely and vulnerable. But that was utter nonsense, she told herself fiercely. He didn't know the meaning of those words.

She felt wretched as she made her way to her bedroom. She was aware of Lane's brooding stare following her until she closed the door behind her.

The only sound in the room was the frantic unsteady rhythm of her heart as she went through the motions of getting ready for bed like a robot. When she crawled in between the sheets, her eyes were wide open. She tossed and turned the entire night trying to outrun her torturous thoughts.

She woke up with a severe headache and a dull listlessness. She forced herself to get out of bed and shower. There were a few things she had to take care of today—she had to see her mother and pay a visit to the store to let Sally and Ron know she was home.

Although the rain had stopped, it was still cold and dreary. She chose a pair of dark brown corduroy pants with a leather belt and a long-sleeved brown and orange striped silk blouse. Even after putting on her makeup, she didn't feel much better.

She walked by Lane's room on her way to the dining room. The door was closed.

During a lonely breakfast of toast and coffee, she

reflected on her situation. She was destined for a few more months of upheaval and turmoil, and she might as well resign herself to that fact. Jamie's trial was due to begin in a few weeks, her job certainly had its complications and the inevitable and final breakup of her marriage was gradually coming to pass.

She lost her appetite completely. Pushing aside her plate, she poured herself another cup of coffee. She walked to the hall closet and threw her coat around her shoulders, grabbed her coffee and was on her way out when the door opened abruptly. She and Lane almost ran into each other.

"Oh!" Paige gasped as she jumped out of the way. The coffee spilled on her boots and down the front of Lane's rumpled suit.

Her heart stopped beating, and she felt sick to her stomach. Obviously, Lane hadn't been home all night.

"Paige! Don't look like that," he rasped. "It's only coffee. It'll come clean, I promise you." His glance flickered over his suit lapels and he smiled fleetingly.

A sob rose in her throat. *He thinks I'm upset because of the coffee,* she screamed to herself. *Where have you been all night?* She wanted to demand an answer, but she didn't care. She just kept staring at him, a dazed look on her face.

"Paige, what's the matter? Are you all right?" His voice held concern.

She shook her head as if to clear it. "I'm—I'm fine. You—you caught me off guard, that's all," she mumbled, refusing to look at him.

He hesitated. "Where were you going?" he asked quietly.

"To Mother's," she answered weakly.

"I see."

At the tired, forlorn note in his voice, she turned slowly to face him and studied him intently. Not only were his clothes rumpled, his eyes were bloodshot and bleary. He looked like he was about to fall on his face.

"Where have you been?" she blurted out in panic. "Has something happened?" Her jealousy had now turned into concern.

Expelling a weary sigh, Lane said bleakly, "I've had one hell of a long night." He strode past her, throwing himself down heavily onto the couch. Paige turned and followed him, sitting tentatively on the edge of the nearest chair. "This merger business has gotten completely out of hand." He paused, rubbing the back of his neck.

She waited patiently for him to continue.

"Your boss's insistence that he can outbid me for the stores is a constant thorn in my side." His voice was harsh.

She asked, choosing her words with care, "Do you—you think he's really smuggling?"

His dark eyes flared. "I know damn well he is! I learned through my contacts in Antwerp that he is definitely involved up to his ears, but I still have to prove it."

Paige pressed her lips together.

"There's no way I'm going to allow that rotten

scoundrel to cut me out, especially with money from smuggled diamonds.''

"Lane,'' she said, licking her lips, ''I don't think I...''

His eyes darkened. ''Yes, you can!'' he told her coldly.

Seeing the hurt look that crossed her face, he softened his tone. ''Paige, I need your help.'' His eyes pleaded with her. ''Surely you don't approve of what he's doing?'' He lifted his dark brows. ''Even if I weren't involved, you must know that what he's doing is wrong and shouldn't be allowed to continue.''

Paige sighed. ''I know. But it's just that I don't know where to start, what to do or anything.'' She began pacing the floor in agitation.

''I want you to keep in mind the word 'submarined.' That's the key.'' He paused, taking in her puzzled frown. ''It's a New York dealers' term meaning someone is engaged in smuggling diamonds. So, if you hear the word mentioned, you'll know you're on to something.''

Paige still looked doubtful.

''Don't worry about it. Just keep your eyes and ears open and I'm sure you'll come up with something concrete we can use. Wallace is sure to become careless.''

''What about Sally? Shall I tell her?''

Lane shot her a quick look. ''By all means, tell her. She may be our best contact.''

Paige looked doubtful. ''I don't know. She and Ron are pretty tight.'' She paused, knitting her brows. ''Although she's certainly aware of his peculiar behavior of late. We've discussed it many times, and she's as puzzled by it as I am.''

"Good," he replied. "We'll take it from there.''

He seemed less weary now to her. Perhaps he had been dreading approaching her again about Ron.

An awkward silence had fallen on the room as Paige felt his eyes resting on her intently. She colored as she felt his glance drop lower, lingering on the cleft between her breasts, barely visible beneath her open-necked blouse. He abruptly turned his head, staring broodingly out the window.

Paige ran a tongue over her dry lips. "I need to be going." Her voice was breathless. She paused, infusing a firm tone into it. "After I stop by Mother's and Jamie's, I'm going to run by the store and see Sally a minute."

Lane stood in front of her, his legs slightly apart, regarding her with narrowed eyes. "Will you be gone long?''

Paige moved toward the door. "I don't know. Why?'' she asked softly.

Lane flexed his shoulder muscles tiredly. "No reason...''

Paige turned abruptly and walked out the door, slamming it shut behind her.

The morning spent at her mother's was pleasant in spite of her tangled emotions. She found her brother in good spirits, struggling to make up missed exams at school, and still on his best behavior. Katherine seemed glad to see her, although she pumped her with questions about Jamie's forthcoming trial. Paige was unable to answer any of them, since she and Lane hadn't discussed the trial at all. She assured her mother that as soon as she found out something, she would let her know.

As soon as Paige could, she left and made her way to the Galleria store. Using her key, she let herself in through the back door.

The first person she encountered was Sally. She stared at Paige for a moment as if she were seeing a ghost. Then rolling her eyes skyward, she exclaimed, "Oh, Paige! Am I ever glad to see you!"

Nine

Paige grinned, eyeing her friend closely. "Let me guess why I was missed. Has my friend, Mrs. Frazier, been giving you trouble?" She inclined her head.

Sally moved quickly, hugging Paige. Stepping back, she laid her hand across her chest. "It's with heartfelt sincerity I welcome you back. You can't imagine how wild it's been around here." Her eyes danced impishly.

Paige smiled. "I'm not at all surprised. But I'm glad to be back. I missed you, too." She paused, dropping her briefcase on her desk. "Is Ron here yet? I sure need to talk to him."

Sally rolled her eyes upward. "Well, he's not here today. And thank God for small favors."

Paige arched an eyebrow in puzzlement at Sally's vehemence toward their boss.

"Believe it or not, he's still acting like an old bear with a sore paw." Sally pouted. "Actually, he's been much worse since you went back to Lane and took off for Belgium."

Paige frowned. "I know he wasn't exactly thrilled about my going back to Lane, but he's been out of sorts for so long…" She shrugged hopelessly. "Who's to say what's contributed to his strange behavior the most?''

Sally's expression was mutinous. Placing her hands on her hips, she exclaimed, ''Well, I for one have about had it! Now that you're home, we ought to confront Ron and find out what's going on!''

Paige hunched her shoulders and sat down at her desk. ''It won't be necessary to talk to him,'' she replied in a dull voice. ''I'm almost positive I know what's troubling our errant boss.''

Sally shot her a quick glance, her eyes widening. ''You do! Don't keep me in suspense, tell me. Whatever it is, it must be bad. Your tone sounds ominous.''

Paige heaved a sigh. ''It is. But before I go into it, how about my treating you to lunch? I was at Mother's earlier, but I wasn't hungry then.''

''Okay. Just let me tell the girls up front and I'll be ready.''

They decided to stick with their usual haunt—the soup and sandwich shop close to the Galleria. They were escorted to their favorite booth and ordered immediately.

Sally wrinkled her pert nose. ''Do you realize I haven't even asked you about your trip to Belgium nor your return to married life.'' She scrutinized Paige closely. ''I'd much rather hear about the last one first, if you don't mind.'' She grinned wickedly.

Paige smiled in return, but she wasn't sure the smile ever reached her eyes. ''I'm making out all right.'' She swallowed a painful lump in her throat. ''I can't and won't pretend everything is a bowl of cherries, because it isn't. But Lane and I reached an agreement we can both live with, so far," she lied.

Sally noted the tense lines around Paige's mouth and forced herself to remain quiet; she certainly didn't intend to bring her friend any more pain and hurt.

Making an attempt to lighten the mood, Paige sucked in her breath and, with all the enthusiasm she could muster, said, "We had a great time in Belgium. We took a lot of pictures and slides of the country-side." She laughed. "And everything else for that matter."

"It must be a great place to visit," Sally chimed in, her eyes dancing.

"Oh, it is. As soon as we get our pictures, I'll bring them to the office for you to see."

Sally chuckled. "Good! Because that'll be the closest I'll ever get to Belgium. Not meaning to change the subject, but I'm dying to hear about Ron..."

Paige bit her lower lip. "Yes, that! Well, there's no way to paint a rosier picture, so I might as well come right out with it." She paused as the waiter brought their food. When they were alone once again, she went on bluntly. "Lane is almost one hundred percent sure that Ron is involved in diamond smuggling out of Antwerp into New York."

Sally gasped! "Are you serious?"

Paige shook her head. "Unfortunately I am. Lane expects me to see what I can learn about the whole sordid mess." She protested helplessly. "I'm at a loss as to where and how to begin. Do you know anything?"

"No," Sally responded in a shocked voice. "I sure don't, but I knew something was going on. I can assure you, though, nothing showed up in the books. If he's making big money on the side, he's sure not putting it in the bank."

Paige expelled a sigh. "Well, I'm going to be working one or two days a week for a while, so maybe he'll give himself away sooner or later."

"Oh, boy! I don't want to be around when you tell Ron you're cutting your working hours. Good luck!"

Paige smiled ruefully. "You can't imagine how much I dread it." She grimaced. "Lane doesn't want me to work full time. Ron won't tolerate it. He may fire me."

"Huh!" Sally challenged. "He wouldn't be that stupid. You're one reason his business is booming." She paused, cocking her head to one side. "Did you by any chance notice the stack of messages from clients waiting for your call?"

Paige frowned. "No—as a matter of fact, I didn't. I guess subconsciously I just couldn't cope with it all right now."

"Well, just remember, I'll be around all the time," Sally assured her, "so I'll do anything I can to bring all this to a head." She sighed. "If Lane's allegations turn out to be right, a lot of us will be looking for another job."

After accompanying Sally back to the office, Paige decided to stay and sort out the mess on her desk. It was five-thirty before she unlocked her car and found herself in the middle of rush-hour traffic on her way to Lane's apartment. She couldn't bring herself to call it home. She clutched the steering wheel tightly in utter frustration.

When she let herself into the apartment, it was strangely quiet. Then she remembered that it was Joseph's night off. She had removed her coat and was heading toward the kitchen to fix herself something to drink, when she looked up and saw Lane standing in the doorway to the den, unclothed except for a towel bound loosely around his narrow waist.

She halted, her eyes glued to the rivulets of water that lay glistening amidst the dark hairs on his chest. Her eyes traveled downward to his naval, so hauntingly familiar to her lips and tongue. A sob caught in her throat as her knees threatened to buckle beneath her.

She fought to control her emotions and her facial features at the same time.

"I...I..." she began, looking around the room. She must look at something besides *him!*

"I heard you come in as I was getting out of the shower," Lane muttered indistinctly. He coughed. "Where've you been?"

Although his tone was soft, his eyes were hard. He expected an answer.

She turned, covering the short distance to the kitchen. Her legs still felt weak. "Well, let's see. I've been to Mother's. I've been to lunch with Sally. And I've worked—sorted through mail, made a few phone calls—that type of thing."

"I was beginning to get worried," he told her heavily.

"You were?" she mumbled softly, averting her head. Her heart was thumping so loudly that she was sure he could hear it. She kept her hands busy filling a glass with ice and pouring Coca-Cola into it until the glass was full.

He remained still. She had a first-hand view of his glowing physique no matter which way she turned. She could tell from the smile playing around the corner of his mouth that he was very aware of the effect he was having on her.

She was addicted to his touch, his kiss and the healthy demands of his powerful body, and he knew it. In bed, they were perfectly suited. Anywhere else, they butted heads like two charged-up bulls.

He was in no hurry to remove his unclothed body. Leaning carelessly against the door frame, he announced in a lazy voice, "I've been out to The Woodlands with a real estate agent, looking at houses. I know I must have looked at twenty if I looked at one." He paused, securing his towel, which was showing signs of slipping.

Paige averted her eyes quickly. She felt cold beads of perspiration break out across her upper lip.

"You haven't heard a word I've said, have you?" Lane demanded, breaking sharply into her thoughts.

Paige couldn't prevent the pink color from invading her cheeks. "No, I haven't. What did you say?" she asked apprehensively.

"I said," he stressed, mockery edging his voice,

"that I chose about ten houses out of the twenty for you to look at and see what you think about them."

Why is he so insistent upon buying a home? she wondered to herself. She hadn't really believed she would follow through with it or she would have black-balled the idea when he had first mentioned it.

"Paige, for God's sake, will you please pay attention to me," Lane exploded. "I feel as if I'm talking to a damned mummy. What's the matter with you anyway? Are you sick?" His eyes narrowed as he stalked closer, like a panther moving in on his prey. He paused in front of the bar, scanning her face intently.

Paige compressed her lips bitterly, disillusionment threatening to swamp her. Forcing a calmness she was far from feeling into her voice, she declared, "I think it's rather foolish to buy a house when our time together is limited, don't you?"

Lane's dark eyes bored into her. "No, I don't happen to think it's foolish," he ground out crossly. "I think the judge will look upon the decision with favor. It'll get Jamie out of the city and away from bad influences and put all types of recreational activities practically at his back door." He was terribly miffed with her and showed it.

She died a little further on the inside upon hearing those words. She should have known the idea of a home was not for them, but was just a means to an end—just another part of the bargain.

Paige swallowed with apparent difficulty. "All right," she acquiesced with a shrug of her tired shoulders. "Whenever you want me to go with you, I'll be ready."

"Well, I wouldn't get too excited about it, if I were you," he told her sarcastically.

Paige pressed her lips together. "What do you want me to do," she snapped irritably, "jump for joy?"

The harsh intake of his breath disturbed the silence between them.

Lane's gaze slid over Paige almost indifferently, contemptuously. "No," he expelled roughly, "I don't want you to do one damn thing!"

With those words, he turned and headed toward his room.

"What's that supposed to mean?" she shouted at his retreating back.

"You figure it out!" he flung over his shoulder as he slammed the door to his room.

Paige gripped the glass of Coke in her hand so tightly the glass shattered into a thousand pieces. She watched with horrified eyes as the blood formed a deep puddle on the counter.

For a second time in her life, Paige fainted.

When she came to, the foul smell of anesthetic drifted to her nose, causing her eyes to water and burn. She cried out as she raised her left arm and saw the bandage that practically covered her lower arm. Her cry of anguish brought Lane and a nurse running to her side.

"Dammit nurse, help her! Is she in pain?" Lane's disturbed voice finally penetrated her drugged senses.

She opened her eyes wide and took in her husband's haggard appearance.

She smiled wanly, trying to show him that she was all right. It was a shock to her to see the white bandaged hand glaring back at her.

"Shhh! Calm down Mr. Morgan. She's just fine." Pushing Lane aside, the nurse coaxed Paige softly. "Now, Mrs. Morgan, I want you to sit up on the side of the table for me." She positioned herself on one side of Paige and beckoned for Lane to move to the other side.

"As we help you up, I want you to breathe deeply and the dizziness will pass much faster."

Paige managed to do as she was told and after a moment the room ceased to whirl in front of her. Lane became a stationary object welded to her side.

"Thank God," he rasped, lifting his eyes heavenward.

For a moment Paige could have sworn she saw tears, but thrust the notion aside as an hallucination.

She looked down and noticed she was fully clothed in her pants and blouse, but was minus her shoes. She wiggled her toes, causing Lane's eyes to drop downward.

He smiled self-consciously. "As you can see, I didn't take time even to grab your shoes. I'm lucky it's not very cold today, or we might have added pneumonia to your problems."

"What about my hand?" she questioned, using the tip of her tongue to wet her parched lips.

Perspiration dotted his forehead and upper lip.

"You cut a deep gash across the center, which required about fifteen stitches."

Her stomach turned at the thought.

"Paige, I can't even turn my back on you," he declared. "I shudder to think what would have happened if I hadn't been nearby both times." He smiled teasingly to lighten the mood. "Maybe the answer would be to tie you to my side, with just enough rope to let you walk, and to do one other thing, of course," he whispered for her ears alone.

Paige felt a burning heat coursing through her body. She simply couldn't understand this man who cajoled her, teased her, petted her with words and looks, but raked himself over the coals for making love to her.

"Paige, I think you ought to remain in the hospital overnight." His face kept its worried look. "What do you think, nurse?" he questioned, turning toward the white-clothed figure busily working across the room.

Before the nurse could reply, Paige spoke up, "Please, Lane, I want to go home," she announced with a surge of strength. "I feel fine now. My hand's not even sore." She smiled as she moved her hand to reassure him.

"Honey, since it's already eight o'clock, don't you think you really should stay?" It was evident by the raspy tone of his voice that he was still upset.

"Please, I feel all right. I want to go home." Her voice quivered in spite of her effort to keep it steady. She was loath to admit even to herself that she didn't feel well, but she didn't want to spend the night in the hospital.

After paying the emergency room bill, Lane picked her up in his arms and carried her to the car. Paige was nestled against his muscled physique before a protest rose to her lips. She found herself being placed in the front seat as if she were made of porcelain glass.

"Are you comfortable?" he asked huskily as he drove through the night.

Paige glanced toward him, taking in the tightly clenched jaw and deeply etched lines at the side of his mouth. Impulsively she leaned across the seat and rested her uninjured hand on his thigh. She felt the muscle jump and then quiver as she said with confidence, "I know you don't believe me, but I feel just fine. When the damp night air hit my face, it revived me. Of course," she added hesitantly, "I feel totally and irrevocably embarrassed for having pulled such a stupid stunt, again!"

"Well, if you're asking me to dispute your choice of words, you're looking at the wrong person." The brief smile he flashed her took the sting out of his words. "Tonight you aged me even more. When we get home, I want to show you I have very little, if any, dark hair left."

She smiled at his attempt to lighten the mood. She was lucky it was her left hand she had cut. She could still work.

As if he could read her mind, Lane said suddenly, "I don't want you to worry about going to work any time soon. I'll call Wallace tomorrow and tell him."

Paige's expression became bleak. "No. Please

don't. I'm sure I'll even feel like working a little to-morrow."

"I don't think…"

"I promise I won't overdo it," Paige cut in abruptly. "If my hand starts hurting, I'll come home. I promise."

Lane sighed wearily. "All right." By the tone of his voice, Paige guessed he wasn't happy with her decision.

"Lane?" Her tone was drowsy.

"Yes?" he answered indulgently.

"Why didn't you ask me about Sally this after-noon?"

"I don't know what you mean." He sounded puzzled.

"I told you I had lunch with Sally," her voice sounded impatient even to her own ears, "and you didn't even bother to ask if I'd found out anything concerning Ron from her."

He shrugged. "So? I figure you would've told me if you'd heard anything different." He paused for a moment, the silence deepening. "I trust you, Paige. I know I can depend on you to do what's right in this matter. Let's take one day at a time, how about it?"

The following morning Paige wasn't able to go to work, nor during the following weeks. The pain in her hand worsened as it became infected. When the infection was under control, Lane took her to The Wood-lands several times to get her out of the apartment. Gradually, he pushed her into a decision about which house to buy. They also agreed on an apartment close by for her mother and Jamie.

Lane hired a decorator, insisting she check with Paige before any of her ideas were implemented. This merely added to Paige's frustrations. Within two weeks after Lane purchased the house, they were living in it. Although she was delighted with her new surroundings, she cautioned herself over and over not to become attached to the new house, since she wouldn't have the pleasure of living there much longer.

The house itself was a dream home. It had a sunken den with a huge corner fireplace. Glass from ceiling to floor comprised the walls along the back of the house as well as the majority of the front. The rooms were all tastefully furnished and decorated in matching carpets and draperies. The yard was filled with lovely oak trees and tall pines, which could be seen from the deck that extended across the entire back of the house.

Lane hovered over her while she was recuperating. He refused to travel and actually worked very little. Although he behaved like a perfect gentleman, Paige was very aware of his every move. She finally faced the fact that his presence reduced her to a complete wanton.

She often felt his gaze stroke her from afar, but he made no attempt to entice her into his bed. She found herself loving him more and more each day, and even though she didn't understand his moodiness—the sadness that flickered across his eyes—she loved him.

Yet, she knew that he no longer loved her, that he

only desired her and merely needed her help. She knew she would be cast aside as soon as the trial ended and she had passed on the incriminating evidence against Ron.

Paige's heart was heavy. By the time she returned to work, she was withdrawn again.

On her first day back on the job, Ron called her into his office. "How's your hand?" he asked abruptly. "It's not going to interfere with your work is it?"

Her mouth tightened. "No, it's not," she responded in a cool voice, "but I'm not going to be able to work except two or three days a week for a while."

She was prepared for an explosion and when it came, she wasn't surprised.

"What!" he exclaimed harshly. Realizing he had practically shouted, he paused to cough and lowered his voice. "I thought your hand was all right, that it had healed."

Paige lowered her head, looking at her hand. "My hand is fine, Ron." She sighed. "I don't feel as if I can go into the reasons with you right now. I'm willing to make up the days I don't work by working twice as hard while I'm here." She turned her blue eyes on him. "But if you choose to let me go, I'll understand…"

She held her breath as she waited for his decision. If he fired her, she wouldn't be able to gather evidence against him for Lane.

Ron made a weary gesture. "Tell me, are you happy with Morgan?"

"Yes," she answered apprehensively. His abrupt

question concerning her personal life caught her off guard. There was a strained silence.

His mouth twisted as his glance flicked over her. "I hope you know what you're doing."

Paige stiffened. Ignoring his warning, she asked bluntly, "What about my job, Ron?"

Forcing his hands deep into his pants pocket, he turned his back on her. "It's still yours," he said dejectedly.

"Thanks," she scarcely breathed. After another moment of strained silence, she turned and walked quickly out the door and back to her office.

A few days later, as she sat brooding at her desk, she wondered how she would ever keep abreast of all the work. Two days a week was simply not enough time. The phone hadn't stopped ringing since she had walked in the door.

All the ideas she had picked up in Antwerp were unfolding, first on paper, and then in the workroom. The design in front of her at the moment was one of which she was extremely proud. It was technically simple, but when the stones were placed, it would be elegant.

She had created a lady's yellow gold diamond ring with a nugget texture finish. The basic design was a soft dome swirl. She planned to place a carat full-cut diamond in the center surrounded by six small marquise-cut diamonds and six small round diamonds. Each stone would be mounted in individual platinum settings.

She sighed out loud as she laid down her pencil.

Looking at her watch, she noticed it was only three o'clock. For some reason she felt worse than usual today. She decided that what she needed to do was go home, take a nice hot bath and then a nap.

Since she had returned to work, Lane had gone back to his vigorous schedule. As a result, she found herself alone most of the time.

Paige deplored her working conditions, but she felt that she was better off at the store than at home. She was tired these days and she hadn't been sleeping well, even when Lane was home.

Her depression and fatigue were caused by her relationship with Lane. Of course, Jamie's trial looming near, and her failure to come up with any evidence against Ron, also contributed to her hypertension. Since returning to work, she hadn't discovered a shred of evidence against Ron. Her frustration mounted daily. What if Lane was wrong and Ron had come by his money legally to bid against him?

Lane had been out of town for a week and Paige was anxious for his flight to arrive from New York at nine o'clock in the evening.

Deciding she would go home early, she picked up the in-house phone and called Sally. Moments later she found herself on her way home to get ready for Lane's arrival...

Paige had been waiting for Lane to come home for nearly two hours before she began to worry. She shivered, folding her arms together. Only the embers remained in the fireplace. Unfolding her legs from their comfortable position on the couch, she drew her thin nylon robe closer around her and walked to the fireplace.

Her hands gripped the poker, punching the smoldering fire back to life. She stifled a yawn and made her way back to the couch. Her eyes strayed to her watch once again as she gnawed at her lower lip. Lane should have been home long ago. She was fighting to stay awake in spite of her uneasiness.

Instead of coming home and going straight to bed as she had planned, she had worked around the house. She worked in the yard for a while and then repotted several of her house plants. It had been a gorgeous afternoon and she had hated to waste it in bed. For March, the weather was perfect—cool, crisp and clear.

She found that the exercise had made her feel better. She had worked outside until dark. Joseph had prepared her a light meal of ham salad and fruit and after her shower she had retreated to the couch with a book.

She had missed Lane more this time than she had ever thought possible. Was it because their time together was drawing to an end? There was no doubt in her mind that Lane would let her go. Desire and love were two different worlds; now that she desperately wanted his love again, she couldn't settle for less.

With tear stains on her cheeks, she laid her head back against the thick cushions and drifted into an uneasy sleep...

She felt all warm inside. She smiled contentedly to herself as she envisioned Lane inflicting feather-light kisses across her cheek. Slowly opening her eyes, she was startled to find Lane's face close to her own.

"Lane?" she whispered.

The room, aglow with firelight, danced across his haggard and worn face.

"Yes, it's me," he mumbled thickly.

"Why are you so late?" she asked, her voice drowsy.

"The plane was late," he responded softly, his gaze lowering from her face to her breasts, their gentle fullness evident through the sheer material of her robe.

A wild longing surged through her as she saw the hunger in his eyes. He remained leaning above her with both arms positioned on either side. She raised her hand to his face, letting it slide over his hair, around the back of his head, bringing his mouth down to hers.

"Oh, Paige…" The words were torn from him as he laid his lips against the inviting sweetness of hers. She opened her mouth and he filled her with the taste of him. His tongue sought her mouth's inner delights, until she moaned in submission.

When the kiss ended, he dropped down on his knees in front of her, wrapped his arms around her and kissed her again. Separating, after a long burning kiss, Lane pressed his head against her breast, listening to the rapid beat of her heart.

He closed his hand over her breast, fondling, caressing, kneading. "Soft, so soft," he muttered in a throaty whisper.

"Lane..." she whispered, her senses drugged, "I—we—shouldn't."

He silenced her with his mouth, as his hands were busy freeing her breasts from the confines of her gown and robe. Paige tingled with anticipation as he succeeded in lowering the bodice, causing her breasts to spill.

Groaning, he raised himself off his knees, never removing his eyes from her velvet smoothness before him. He reached for her hand and gently pulled her from the couch. Leading her by the hand, he dropped to his knees on the rug in front of the fire. Paige had no choice but to follow. Her senses were controlled by his potent touch. She would give herself to him and take this moment with her and savor it for the rest of her life.

Lane touched her lovingly. His hand cupped a breast bringing it upward to meet his mouth. He stroked it, kissed it, inhaled it until she was wild with longing. He moved from one breast to the other until they were both swollen and taut from his lips.

Her hand went to his tie. She pulled the knot forward until it was loosened enough to come undone. Then she undid the buttons of his shirt down to his belt buckle.

From there, he took over. He raised himself to his full height and removed the remainder of his clothing. He stood naked before her, unable to deny how much he desired and worshipped her. He dropped to his knees once again in front of her, lifting her up just enough to dislodge and remove the shimmering softness of her robe, followed by her gown. She was soon disarrayed before him. The firelight rippling across her body only heightened his insatiable appetite for her.

Paige looked up at him. "Here…?" she questioned, uncertainty crowding her voice.

"Yes, here," Lane ground out in a guttural voice as he laid her gently down on the rug.

Her lily white body lay exposed to his smoldering gaze. He positioned himself alongside her, propping his head on his arm, enabling him to have full access to her lips. Paige ran her hands along the hard muscles in his back forcing him closer as he pressed his firm mouth to hers. He sipped, nibbled and tasted the almost unbearable sweetness of her lips.

She reveled in his feel, touch and smell and moaned, moving her head from side to side as his mouth sought her breasts. He kissed and nuzzled them until they were full and tender.

When he lowered his head and dipped his tongue into her naval, she cried aloud, "Yes, Lane, yes! Don't stop!"

She heard his warm chuckle as he continued to bring her to spiraling heights of ecstasy. Her quivering reactions to his delving tongue only served to increase his passion for her.

Paige knew how to please him in turn. Long ago, he had taught her how to render him mindless with her mouth and hands. When he had reached his limit, and couldn't take any more, his hand moved lower, seeking her inner thighs, parting them with insistent fingers.

Her shuddering response and parting invitation of her limbs encouraged him to remain on his side facing her, where his eyes probed hers as he continued to stroke and tease. His fingers felt like hot pokers scorching her skin everywhere they probed...touched. Paige cried out in utter delight as Lane took her. Clutching him, she met him, taking him deeper, deeper within her.

They remained thus, each retaining a part of the other. It wasn't long until their breathing became normal. Paige slipped into drowsy contented slumber as she lay folded within his arms.

Ten

Paige awakened, immediately aware that something was different. She looked around the room, taking in the unfamiliar surroundings. Her eyes widened as they landed on the man's clothing strewn about the room.

Her heart sank when she heard Lane singing at the top of his lungs, his voice mingling with the splattering water of the shower.

She groaned and turned back against the pillows, pulling the sheet with her. When had Lane carried her to bed? Why to his room?

Not able to answer either question, Paige sat up, swung her legs around and sat on the side of the bed. She flinched, as the sudden action made her aware of her sore limbs.

She felt herself grow hot remembering what had taken place between them the previous night. *But I don't regret anything,* she told herself.

Yawning, she scanned the room again, looking for a sign of her gown and robe. There was none. With a sigh, she rose and walked across the room and grabbed Lane's dress shirt from where it lay in a crumpled heap on the floor.

She was fastening the last button when Lane came

sailing through the bathroom door. He stopped short when he saw her standing in the middle of the room.

A slow smile played around the corners of his mouth as he took in the enchanting picture she made with her hair in total disarray about her shoulders, his shirt barely reaching the tips of her knees. Hot color rushed up her neck and into her face as his smile deepened into a grin. He stood nonchalantly in front of her, staring, enjoying her plight. She smiled back at him, her hands reaching to sweep her tumbled locks away from her face.

He laughed outright, securing the ever present towel around his waist.

Pulling herself up to her full height, Paige braced her hands on her hips. "What's so damned funny?" she snapped, turning to remove her gaze from his near nudity.

"Absolutely nothing," he stated softly, humor still lacing his voice.

She tilted her head to one side, eyeing him suspiciously. "Well, in that case, I'm off to my room."

"What's your hurry?" he demanded calmly. He reached out to hold her.

She stared at him uncertainly. "I—I need to—to shower," she answered him breathlessly.

"What's wrong with my shower?" His eyes held her.

"Please, Lane," she murmured, "don't tease me."

He sighed. "I'm not teasing you. But since you're as nervous as a cat on a hot tin roof, I'll behave."

She smiled, her face relaxing a little.

"However," he went on to say, his brilliant eyes searing, "I want you to give serious thought to our sharing the same bedroom."

Paige held her breath.

"And the same bed," he told her huskily.

She forced herself to look at him as he watched her intently, waiting...

She licked her lips with her pink-tipped tongue. "Lane, I..." Words failed her. She hated telling him no, because in all honesty, she wanted to share his bed. She loved being a part of him. *But would this be wise?* she asked herself.

"Please, Paige, don't say no," he told her huskily, "at least not right this minute. Will you think about it?"

"All right," she responded, although her words were barely audible.

She felt rather than saw his shoulders sag in relief as she turned around, making her way to the door like a deer bolting from a hunter.

When she reached her room, she flung off Lane's shirt, tossed it on the floor and headed for the shower. The water felt blissful as it pounded against her skin before running down her body, taking with it Lane's scent and touch.

As she vigorously soaped her body, turmoil, mixed with apprehension and anticipation, confused her thoughts. Already, she knew what her answer would be to Lane's offer—she would say yes. If she could lock more nights like the one they had just shared next to her heart, she would indeed collect enough love to last her a lifetime.

By the time she washed her hair and started to dress, Lane was leaving to go to his office. She heard his car back out of the drive as she tried to decide what to wear on this mild March day. She finally chose a navy blue cotton poplin jumper with a long-sleeved silk blouse. After a light breakfast, she, too, headed for work.

An hour later, Paige had her work apron on and was about to go into the jewelry workshop when the telephone on her desk buzzed. Sighing, she crossed the room and lifted the receiver rather absently. "Yes."

"Paige…? Is that you?"

"Yes, it's me," she responded lightly.

Lane's velvet chuckle over the phone almost caused her heart to stop. "Well, for a moment I wasn't too sure. Did I interrupt anything? Is Wallace there?"

"The answer is no to both questions. I was on my way to the workroom to pour some molds."

"I won't keep you long, then. John Allen called a moment ago and wants us to have dinner with him and his wife tonight. Any objections?"

"Who's John Allen?" The name had a familiar ring to it.

"You've never met him, but it's an important invitation. I'll tell you more about it later."

"Well, in that case," Paige declared roundly, "I'll leave work early and go to the beauty shop."

She heard his warm chuckle through the receiver. "You women and your vanity!"

"Huh!" she retaliated, "Men are twice as..."

"I'll see you later, honey," Lane interrupted, amusement in his voice. "Don't be late."

The receiver buzzed in her ear. She stood holding it for a moment, a warm glow around her heart. This feeling remained with her as she worked, pouring one mold after the other. Even Ron's gruff inquiry about several clients couldn't dispel her mood.

She noted, however, that Ron looked even more haggard than usual. He remained behind closed doors of late, which puzzled her. She had questioned Sally several times about the person or persons Ron was spending an inordinate amount of time with in his office. Sally had merely shrugged, saying whoever it was always left through Ron's private office.

Now as she walked down the hall toward the workroom, she noticed his door was closed again. She must remember to mention Ron's strange behavior to Lane.

It didn't take Paige long to pour the molds and place them in their proper place to dry. If she had time after her beauty appointment, she would return to the store for a little while. Or better still, she would stop by one of the other stores and check on it. There weren't enough hours in the day to properly do her job, she decided.

Anticipating the evening ahead of her, Paige strolled into the beauty salon. She sat down in the lounge area to await her turn and was leafing through a magazine when she heard her name being called.

She looked up quickly not having recognized the

voice. Her eyes widened as they encountered the pet-ulant and bold stare of Jill Taylor.

Paige's heart plunged. Her intuition told her there was trouble brewing. However, she let none of her inner chaos show as she politely acknowledged Lane's former mistress with a half smile.

"Darling," Jill drawled, as she sat down beside Paige on the small couch. "I'm so glad I ran into you today. It'll save me a trip to Lane's office."

Paige stiffened at the mention of her husband. "How can I help you?" she asked through tight lips. She waited with dread as the scarlet-mouthed woman opened her purse and delved her hand into it.

This gave Paige a chance to study her adversary. As usual, Jill Taylor was a epitome of glamour and elegance. Her clothes were tailored to perfection, hug-ging her voluptuous body in all the right places, and there wasn't a hair out of place on her head. But to Paige's knowledge, Jill didn't patronize this particular beauty salon.

"Oh, here it is," Jill said breathlessly in her honey-toned voice. "For a moment I was afraid I hadn't brought it with me," she cooed sweetly as she brought her hand out of her purse, her tightly clenched fist clutching an object Paige couldn't see.

Paige's patience was stretched to the limit. It was all she could do to keep from reaching over and slap-ping Jill's smug, beautiful face. She couldn't believe that she was allowing herself to be intimidated by this scheming woman. Paige met Jill's stare with what she hoped was an air of nonchalance.

"Would you please return this to Lane for me?" Jill asked sweetly. "He left it at my apartment one night this past week."

Paige felt herself bristle at the implication behind those confident words. She forced herself to look down at Jill's outstretched hand.

There lay the solid gold money clip she had given Lane for Christmas. She recoiled from touching it as if it were poisonous.

For a moment her facade slipped and panic gripped her insides. "Where did you get that?" she hissed, still refusing to take it from Jill's hand.

"I told you darling," Jill responded, her voice heavy with assurance, "He left it at my apartment."

"I don't believe you!" Paige retorted sharply, but there was a slight waiver in her voice.

Jill detected it and played on it. "Oh, yes, you do," she replied with self-assurance. "Think about it for a moment. Where else would I have gotten it, if Lane hadn't left it at my apartment?"

Uncertainty and frustration coursed through Paige's body. But she wasn't about to let this woman see how devastated she was at learning of Lane's deceit. No, she absolutely couldn't sink that low. Paige squared her shoulders and reached for the money clip.

"Thank you, Miss Taylor," she said coolly, her head held high, "I'll see that he gets it."

With those carefully uttered words, Paige managed to stand up on her shaky legs and insouciantly made her way out the door into the bright afternoon sunshine.

As soon as she rounded the corner of the building, she halted. Leaning back against the brick wall, she strove for composure.

Again she had been duped. She should have known that she and Lane could never make it together. There were too many scars and tears in the past and too many unsolved problems in the future. She had been chasing a rainbow.

Hot burning tears streamed down her face into her mouth. The cloud had finally descended, showing her that the rainbow was nothing but a mirage, like her marriage. She decided that she would fulfill her bargain with Lane and then pack her bags and leave him. She still had her work. Once, it had been the most important thing in her life—it could be again.

Taking a deep breath, Paige struck out in the direction of her car. An hour later she found herself alone in her bedroom, trying desperately to get hold of herself. Her self-confidence had ebbed considerably.

No matter how hard she chastised herself, she abhorred being used. She didn't understand how Lane could have made such tender love to her after having spent time in Jill's bed.

Lane was due home at any minute and expected her to be ready for their dinner date this evening. She hadn't made any effort to get dressed and didn't intend to. All she had done was pace the floor, with Lane's money clip clasped tightly in her hand.

Shortly, the sound of Lane's whistle vibrating throughout the house announced his presence. She stood still and waited in agonizing dread for the inevitable confrontation.

The soft tap on her bedroom door was followed by the turn of the doorknob. "Paige, I hope you're about ready. I'm..."

He stopped short, narrowing his eyes as he took in Paige's taut figure.

Lane's presence filled the room. She averted her eyes quickly lest he see her pain. She adamantly refused to give him the satisfaction of knowing his actions had hurt her.

"Paige...?"

She kept her back to him, holding her shoulders and body erect. The money clip burned a hole in her hand.

"Why aren't you getting dressed?" he asked, his voice smooth, though critical.

Paige turned toward him, her face pale. "I'm not going," she stated flatly.

Lane lifted his dark brows. "May I ask why not?" Although his outward appearance was calm, she wasn't fooled. She knew that underneath his smooth facade he was angry. He didn't like being defied.

"I don't feel well," she declared coolly. She squeezed the object in her hand so hard she felt it cut into the soft flesh of her palm.

"Come on, Paige, you can do better than that," he bit out savagely. "Remember, I wasn't born yesterday."

She flushed at the veiled contempt behind his words, but nevertheless stood firm. "Think what you like,'' she flung back tonelessly. "But I'm still not going.''

He clenched his jaw. "Paige, what's the matter now?'' he demanded in a blistering tone. "You're the most unpredictable, frustrating woman I know.'' He made a weary gesture as he closed the gap between them.

Paige bolted like a frightened doe. "Don't you dare come any closer to me!'' she cried bitterly.

"Paige, what the…!'' He broke off in midsentence, obviously trying to control his temper. He breathed deeply and in a more calm tone said, "Can't we sit down like two civilized adults and hash out whatever accusation you're harboring against me?''

A sob rose in her throat. "No. I'm through talking.'' Her voice was scarcely audible.

"Well, by God, I'm not!'' he bellowed. "This is a very important dinner engagement tonight and I won't have you ruin it for me.''

"Why, why you…!'' The lump was so large in her throat that she couldn't speak.

"My patience has come to an end with your on-again-off-again attitude. I'm no longer asking, I'm demanding…''

"Demanding!'' Paige broke in hotly. "If that's the case, then I have a demand of my own.''

Lane uttered an expletive.

"Can you explain this?'' she ground out through clenched teeth.

Before Lane could say anything or make a move,

Paige hurled the gold money clip at him. It bounced off his chest with a thud, landing at the tip of his shoe.

His harsh intake of breath was the only sound in the room as he slowly, methodically leaned down and scooped up the shiny object.

Tears edged her thick lashes. As his eyes bore into hers, the contempt she saw there was no longer veiled.

Paige didn't flinch. She stood firm, throwing him a look equal to his own. *Say something!* she screamed at him silently. *Say you didn't leave it there! Say you haven't been near her lately!*

But he said none of these things. In a cold, detached voice, he asked "Do you mind telling me where you got this."

"Don't play innocent with me, Lane Morgan," she flung back at him.

He expelled a rugged breath. "I'm sorry to disappoint you, but I'm not playing innocent with you. Why are you making such a big deal out of it?" He paused, narrowing his eyes. "Surely this money clip isn't the reason you're so strung out? Granted, I shouldn't have misplaced the damn thing, but I certainly intended to find it."

Her disbelieving eyes continued to hold his gaze. "Do you mean you're going to stand there and deny that you left it in Jill Taylor's apartment last week?" she questioned nastily.

His eyes narrowed. "I don't know what you're talking about," he stated, his voice edged with steel.

"Well, I'm sorry, but I don't believe you!" she lashed back at him. "Sweet Jill made it a point to confront me at the beauty salon this afternoon just so she could drop this little bombshell into my lap!''

"And it obviously worked exactly the way she planned it," he expressed wearily. He looked exasperated.

Paige frowned. "What's that supposed to mean? I can't see…"

"Forget it!" he cut in swiftly. "I already have given you all the explanation I'm going to." He paused, dragging his palms down his thighs. "You either trust me or you don't. I'm tired of all this hassle."

She looked at him in disgust. "Really?" she snapped sarcastically, turning away from him in an attempt to hide her frustration and jealousy.

He remained stationary, a cold grimace on his face.

If only she could believe his uncomplicated explanation that he had misplaced the clip—but she couldn't. Jealousy gnawed at her insides. She hated herself for this feeling and felt cheapened to think she would swallow such a flimsy rationalization.

"Paige…?"

She turned toward him, her lips parted.

His eyes darkened. "I still expect you to get dressed and go with me tonight." He glanced down at his watch. "You have exactly one hour before we have to leave."

Her shoulders sagged as she shook her head. "No, Lane. I won't take one step out the door with you."

He folded his arms across his chest, eyeing her dangerously. "Oh, I think you will," he told her firmly. "If I remember correctly, we have a bargain. As Jamie's trial doesn't begin for two days, it's not too late..."

Her face grew shadowed. "Are you threatening me, Lane?"

"Label it whatever you want. But a bargain is a bargain. If I keep mine, you'll sure as hell keep yours. And I consider this dinner date part of the bargain."

With those words he turned and stalked out of the room.

Paige didn't really believe Lane would make good his threat about Jamie, but if she pushed him much further...she shuddered just thinking about the consequences. But she swore she wouldn't allow him to coerce her into doing his bidding.

As the time to leave drew near, however, she took Lane's threat to heart, deciding to comply with his demand. Jamie's trial date was too near. According to Lane, the case was shaping up extremely well. She couldn't handle the thought of anything going awry at this late date.

It was with hostility and bitterness that she dressed for the evening. She wore a halter-necked gown of burgundy silk which clung to her curves. She brushed the long silky strands of her hair away from her face, securing them with her diamond-edge combs. A mauve-colored shawl completed her outfit.

The evening passed in a complete blur for Paige. It was apparent that she did and said the right things, because she failed to incur any harsh looks from Lane. He was his usual urbane self, charming both Mr. and Mrs. Allen with amusing anecdotes. The fixed smile on her face saw her through the ordeal, and from all accounts, the Allens seemed taken with her delicate beauty.

Although the Allens held Lane in high esteem, the albatross of Ron's bid still hung around his neck. During the evening, Mr. Allen never came right out and told Lane he would take his bid. To Paige, it seemed that her boss remained very much in the running.

At the end of the evening, they drove home in strained silence. Paige, upon reaching her room, let out a sigh of relief as she kicked off her shoes. She had felt like a bird trapped in a gilded cage during the entire evening. The moment she reached up to undo the fastening on her dress, there came a soft rap on the door. Her hand stilled in midair.

"Lane?" she asked hesitantly as she crossed the room on unsteady legs.

"Yes, it's me," she heard him murmur through the door.

Paige's heart skipped a beat. *What does he want now?* she asked herself. With trembling fingers, she slowly turned the knob.

Their eyes met for a fraction of a second, and then Lane thrust a small object into her hand. Paige glanced down at it as her hand closed around a tape recorder. Then she looked up at him in surprise.

"Keep it in your purse, and if you hear anything the least bit suspicious, put it on tape," he told her blandly.

"All right," she sighed heavily as she saw her hopes disintegrate before her eyes. "But so far, I've heard nothing. The only thing out of the ordinary is Ron's habit of staying behind closed doors.''

"Really? How long has that been going on?'' His smooth tone did nothing to belie his interest.

"Oh, I'd say not more than a couple of weeks,'' she returned hesitantly.

"Well, I feel he's backed himself into a tight corner, which means he'll be making a mistake.'' His voice was hard. "I aim to make sure he'll be out of the jewelry business forever.''

Paige shivered.

After Lane left, she felt worse than ever. She readied herself for bed and finally settled in for what she assumed would be a long sleepless night.

The next few days were busy for Paige. The trial began two days after their dinner engagement. She kept a hectic schedule driving to and from the courthouse and work. On the days she didn't work, she took her mother with her. Katherine was a bundle of nerves, and Paige tried to spend as much time with her as she possibly could.

Jamie was holding up well. Because of his continued good behavior, his attorneys were very encouraged.

Paige saw very little of her husband. He slipped into the courtroom whenever he could. Business problems kept him tied down and the merger wasn't settled. So the tension between her and Lane didn't lessen. After the bitter words concerning the money clip had passed between them, they remained as aloof as strangers.

Paige made herself go to work as often as possible to try and get concrete evidence against Ron. Time was a crucial factor now. Lane was convinced that Ron would make a mistake at this time if he was going to make one at all.

Everyone in the store knew that Mr. Allen expected Ron to come up with the money within the next few days. If not, Allen's stores were going to Lane.

Being on the run as much as she was and being under such pressure, Paige began losing weight. Her features became drawn, and her sleeping habits worsened. She realized her ill health was brought on mostly by her frozen relationship with her husband. She longed for his comfort and his support. She longed for his touch. She told herself she was a fool but she still wanted him. Jealousy kept gnawing away at her insides. If he would only give her a reasonable explanation of how Jill could have gotten his money clip, she would be in his arms in a second.

When they were together she could feel his eyes on her. But when she would turn toward him, the shutter always fell back into place, blocking out his innermost thoughts and feelings. He seemed to be unable to forgive her for doubting him. *Yet, how could I have done otherwise,* she asked herself, *when the evidence was so strong against him?*

She had decided to work late since Lane was out of town and wasn't due to return until later that night. She abhorred going home to the empty house. It was cold and lonely without Lane. Even with the strain between them, she preferred it when he was at home.

Sighing, she forced herself to return to the matter at hand. She must make an effort to clear her desk of all its paperwork. But unwanted thoughts kept intruding. Any day now, a verdict was expected in Jamie's trial. Things were touch and go at the present time. The prosecuting attorney in his summation had raked Jamie over the coals. Katherine had left the courtroom yesterday in tears, and Paige had been shaken herself. Lane, for once, had been there. For the moment, all hostilities had been forgotten, and she had found her hand clasped tightly within his. The goose bumps had danced up and down her arm coming to rest in the lower regions of her stomach. It was all she could do to keep from squirming in her seat.

He wanted her. She loved him. But the tears of yesterday kept intruding, keeping them apart. Neither one made a move toward the other. Only their desires managed to surface during unguarded moments.

It was an hour after closing time. With her desk finally in order, she rose tiredly and made her way to the file cabinet to get her purse. The slamming of a door caused her to stand still. Her heart thumped loudly. Lane had warned her not to stay in the office alone after dark, but she hadn't taken his warning seriously until now.

She silently walked to the door, her purse clutched tightly in her hand. Carefully she turned the knob. She didn't see anyone, but she heard voices and saw the light shining from beneath Ron's door.

She breathed a sigh of relief. Deciding to let him know she was still in the building, she made her way lightly down the carpeted hallway toward his office. The door was slightly ajar and she paused a moment before raising her hand to knock. She wondered if his companion was the phantom visitor, as she and Sally had come to label him.

Paige's hand froze in midair. She ceased breathing for timeless moment as she heard Ron say in a low-keyed but taut voice. "Can I expect the submarined goods tomorrow night?"

Paige's hand flew to her mouth in sudden panic. Fright wrapped its tentacles around her as she slowly opened her purse and drew out the tiny tape recorder. She remained glued to the spot aiming the instrument through the crack in the door.

She didn't know how long she remained in one position. The only thing she was aware of was all the incriminating evidence against Ron and his partner that she was hearing and taping. The whole plan for smuggling the diamonds out of Antwerp to the West was repeated over and over between them until every detail was memorized.

Paige was appalled. According to the plans, Ron's hands wouldn't be dirtied. He was the brains behind the operation and would reap all the benefits without taking any of the actual risks.

When she felt she had enough evidence to completely shatter Ron's world, she turned, forcing herself to walk slowly back toward her office, lest she become careless and give herself away.

She was hurriedly stuffing her briefcase with sketched designs she wanted to work on at home, when she realized she was no longer alone. She stood up slowly, turning to see Ron standing in the doorway staring at the tape recorder blatantly sitting on the top of her desk. In her haste to fill her briefcase to leave, she had forgotten it.

Paige groaned inwardly at her stupidity. She should have rejected returning to her office. By now she could have been well on her way home. Masking her features to appear unperturbed, she smiled coolly in Ron's direction and waited.

He cocked his head to one side, his smile twisted. "My, my, but aren't you the busy little beaver? I didn't know your husband allowed you to work overtime." His tone of voice and manner were both insulting.

She refused to let him intimidate her. "I was just leaving," she told him stonily, totally ignoring his rudeness.

"What's your hurry, now, Mrs. Morgan?" he prodded, a snarl curling his upper lip. His eyes were still focused on the tiny black object on her desk.

A sense of uneasiness overcame her. She told herself to play it cool. The worst Ron could do was erase the tape. She was positive she wasn't in any physical danger. But as he stalked closer to her desk with a menacing look on his face, she became alarmed.

He paused and picked up the recorder and then perched himself on the edge of her desk. He began tossing it up and down in his hands.

Paige bit down on her bottom lip to keep from crying out in fright. She couldn't afford to let him see that she was the least bit interested in his actions.

She was only a hair's-breadth away from Ron. She had been afraid to move. But when he accidentally lost control of the recorder and it landed with a thud on the carpet, Paige bolted like a streak of lightening and scooped it up in her hands.

She clutched it close against her chest and backed away from Ron. Her eyes were wide with uncertainty as she stared at him.

He laughed a cold mirthless laugh as he folded his arms across his chest. He was in no hurry to make his move. "You don't honestly think I'm going to let you leave here with that tape recorder, now do you?" He swung his leg back and forth as his narrowed eyes bored into her.

Paige counted to ten hoping to erase the tension that bound her. She realized she had to get out of the room with the tape. She must do this for Lane.

Forcing her voice to appear as normal as possible under the circumstances, she lied, "Ron, you can't stop me from taking the machine." She paused to re-affirm her hold on it. "Get out of my way."

"You're not going anywhere until you give it to me."

He began to methodically move toward her, his hand outstretched. "Paige, I have no intention of hurting you. All I want is the recorder. Then you can go about your merry way."

He moved closer.

"Stay were you are, Wallace!" Lane commanded

as he strode through the door, violence sparking in his eyes. "If you so much as take another step toward her, I'll break every bone in your body!"

There was no doubt in either of their minds that he would do exactly as he stated.

Her relief was so intense that Paige sagged limply against the nearest wall. Lane strode toward her, never taking his eyes off Ron. With shaking hands she gave him the recorder, which he then slipped into his suit pocket.

They both stared at Ron. His shoulders sagged in defeat. His eyes were glazed in misery.

"You're through, Wallace. Through with smuggling, through in the jewelry business and through in Houston. If I ever catch you anywhere around here or involved in anything connected with jewelry, I'll finish you off."

He paused a moment, letting his words echo in the room.

"And don't think you can get around me or my influence. Because, as you well know, it won't work. By this time tomorrow, every jeweler with any reputation between here, New York and Antwerp will know about you." Lane paused, drawing Paige next to his firm body. "You know," he went on harshly, "we jewelers have a way of punishing our own..."

His last words were the final blow. Ron's face turned as white as a sheet. There were no words to express his utter dejection.

Paige, at Lane's insistence, left her car in the parking lot to be picked up the next morning. As soon as she was settled comfortably in Lane's car, he quickly lowered himself behind the wheel.

He gazed at her and saw the anguish on her face. Her lower lip began to quiver.

With a groan, Lane reached for her and pulled her close to his side.

"Oh, Paige," he murmured thickly, "I'm so sorry about all this mess."

Her warm tears soaked his shirt as he rocked her in his arms.

"It's going to be all right," he assured her. "You go ahead and cry. I don't want you to keep it all bottled up inside."

Paige cried until she was completely spent. She remained in his arms, feeling warm and protected until she eased into a dreamy contentment.

Before she drifted off to sleep, she could have sworn she felt light kisses caress her temple. A smile gently curved her lips. Then she remembered no more...

Eleven

The following morning, Paige overslept. After two cups of hot coffee, she finally had enough energy to take a shower and get dressed.

A few minutes later, she stepped out of the shower and toweled her skin roughly. This bit of exertion left her feeling weak, tired and depressed.

In a little while, the twelve men and women on the jury at Jamie's trial were due to file into the courtroom and deliver their verdict either for or against him. Her obligation to Lane would then be ended, and she would be free to go. *But I don't want to leave him!* she told herself with a cry of anguish. If only he still loved her and would ask her to stay.

She pushed these thoughts aside, realizing they would only enhance her despondency and pain. Right now, she had to finish dressing and make her way downtown as rapidly as possible. Katherine and Jamie needed her.

Although she didn't feel like eating anything, she knew she had to put something in her stomach. A piece of toast sounded good. She had the kitchen all to herself as she buttered some toast and forced it down along with a cup of hot tea.

She was busily cleaning up her mess when a deep voice behind her said, "Are you about ready to go?"

Paige jumped like a frightened rabbit before turning around to face her husband leaning negligently against the door frame. "I wish you wouldn't slither up behind me like that! You nearly scared me to death!"

Lane took in the pallor of her face against the bright color of her dress and his amused expression vanished. His eyes darkened as he swiftly crossed the room to stand next to her.

She braced herself for his touch, but it never came. Instead their gazes locked. A feeling of intense longing surged through her as she dropped her eyes to the tiny razor cut on his chin. The warmth of his presence drew her closer.

"Paige, I—" he began hoarsely as his fingers reached out to cup her chin.

The sharp peal of the phone instantly brought them back to reality. Paige heard Lane's muttered groan as he stepped back abruptly. She shook her head to try and clear her senses.

Lane turned sharply on his heels and strode to the den to answer the phone. She could hear his clipped tone as he talked into the receiver but paid no attention to what was being said. She was too busy fighting to regain her control.

By the time she took several deep breaths to quiet her rapidly beating heart, Lane was once again in the kitchen with her.

Without preamble he said, "That was your Mother.

She and Jamie are already at the courthouse and waiting for us. Rather impatiently, I might add.''

Paige's eyes widened. "Us?"

"Yes, *us*," he replied firmly. "You didn't honestly think I was going to let you go by yourself, did you?" He eyed her closely, his dark brows arched.

She cleared her throat. "No—that is—" She spread her hands. "Well, I didn't really expect you to drive me..." She paused, flashing him a sweet smile. "But, I'm glad you are."

"Well," he said gruffly, tearing his eyes away from her, "we had better get going. Katherine's worked herself into a frenzy, and I told her we would hurry."

Paige breathed deeply before admitting, "I guess I'm about as ready as I'll ever be."

Her legs felt like lead as she moved across the room to precede Lane out the door.

During the hour it took for them to drive, they hardly spoke at all. But she was constantly aware of Lane's presence beside her. From time to time, her eyes drifted toward his face, taking in his jutting brow and smooth, cleanly shaven jaw. She breathed his cologne, making her more aware of his unyielding power over her.

Where is all this going to end? she asked herself. She was positive Lane still desired her. But enough to ask her to stay?

By the time Lane parked the car and walked around to help her out, her thoughts were chaotic. She tried desperately to compose herself.

A frantic Katherine was waiting for them at the entrance to the courtroom. The lawyers had apparently already escorted Jamie to his seat since it was nearly trial time.

Paige tried to ignore the butterflies in her stomach as she turned her full attention to her mother.

Katherine's eyes were glued to the self-assured figure at Paige's side. "Oh, Lane," she cried, clutching at his arm. "I'm so frightened, I'm…" A choked sob claimed her voice.

"Shush!" broke in Lane, in a soft but commanding tone. "Everything's going to be just fine." He drew her arm through his and, with a nod in Paige's direction, escorted them into the room.

Paige heaved a sigh of relief that Lane's apparent hostility toward her mother had been dropped, at least momentarily.

Jamie's eyes searched for them from his seat at the front. Paige saw a smile tug at the corners of Lane's mouth as he winked at Jamie. Her brother's shoulders seemed to relax at Lane's show of confidence.

For the next two hours, Paige sat in animated suspense. Her hand remained firmly enclosed in Lane's as they waited with bated breaths for the bailiff to inform the judge that the jury had reached a verdict.

A short time later, the judge finally received the word that the jury had indeed come to a decision. As the twelve men and women filed into the jury box, Paige dug her nails into the palm of Lane's hand. He didn't flinch even though he must have felt some pain.

In a firm voice, the judge asked, "Foreman, have the jury reached a verdict?"

"Yes, we have, Your Honor," the foreman responded.

The judge turned his eyes toward Jamie. "Will the defendant please rise?"

The only sound in the courtroom was the scrape of Jamie's chair as he pushed it back and stood up.

Hot tears filled Paige's eyes as she saw the terrified expression reflected on her brother's face and in his stance.

She heard Katherine's sob as she, too, noticed her son's fright. Only Lane seemed to be in complete control, remaining patient and confident.

"Will you please read the verdict," the judge ordered.

Paige held her breath.

The foreman swung around to face the judge. "Your Honor, we, the jury, find the defendant guilty as charged. But we recommend that, since it's his first offense, the defendant be treated with leniency."

Paige slumped limply against Lane. She couldn't bear to look at the judge, but she couldn't block out his words. She was afraid of what he would say.

For a moment there was again silence in the room. Then the judge spoke: "In view of what the jury have recommended, I place the defendant Jamie E. McAdams on two years' probation."

It was all Paige could do to keep still.

"I also order," continued the judge, "that the medical bills of the injured parties be paid in full by the defendant's family."

Underneath thick eyelashes, Paige glanced at Lane.

He had already agreed to pay the medical bills of the couple injured in the accident, in addition to giving them a cash settlement. This wasn't part of her bargain with him, but he had nevertheless agreed to make the compensation.

Soon Jamie was ready to leave the courtroom. The trial was finally over and her brother was free to try and make something of himself. Paige was encouraged, since she had seen a change in Jamie during the past few months. Even though Lane hadn't been able to spend a lot of time with him, Jamie knew that Lane was around if he needed him.

As soon as they had walked out of the courtroom into the bright spring day, Lane took them to a casual lunch at a charming Mexican restaurant close by. However, the sight of the food turned Paige's stomach. She only managed to eat a few bites of guacamole salad and some crackers. She felt Lane's questioning gaze on her, but she had no answer for him, so she kept quiet.

Katherine and Jamie followed them home with plans to spend the remainder of the day there. During the early part of the afternoon, it was extremely warm, enabling Lane and Jamie to go in swimming. The pool looked inviting to Paige but she had laughingly refused to be talked into joining the two roughnecks.

Lane swam up to the edge of the pool and pulled on her foot. "What's the matter?" He grinned widely, drawing attention to the lines at the corner of his eyes. "Are you afraid we'll duck you?" he asked her in a playful voice.

"You're exactly right," she stated, returning the grin. "And I don't apologize for it, either."

"You'll be sorry."

"I doubt that. You two sound like a herd of elephants in the water."

"Okay," Lane drawled lazily, "but I'll make you pay for not joining us—later," he added for her ears alone as he swam away on his back.

Hope surged through her as she lay back comfortably on the lounge chair and watched. As the sun beat down on her legs and arms exposed in her sleeveless tee shirt and shorts, she found herself succumbing to drowsiness. Katherine had gone to the guest room to take a nap as soon as they had arrived home.

The evening passed in much the same manner as the afternoon—lazily. Lane barbecued brisket on the outside grill and she and her mother made potato salad and fixed baked beans to go with the meat, and made cheesecake for dessert.

The air crackled with electricity every time Lane's eyes met hers. His dark orbs glittered over her soft curves with a familiarity that raised her blood pressure. A look, a touch, just being together was enough for Paige.

Now, as she sat at her dressing table brushing her hair, the day over, it occurred to her that she hadn't even thanked Lane for making Katherine's and Jamie's day such a happy one.

She laid down her brush, stood up and donned her robe. Before she had second thoughts, she made her way down the hall to Lane's room. Without pausing, she tapped softly on the door.

A hesitant "Come in," followed her knock.

Paige slowly turned the knob and opened the door. The instant she crossed the threshold, her heart leaped to her throat. Lane stood before her clothed only in his underwear. The cotton briefs molded his masculine frame to perfection and his sinewy body was open to her gaze.

"Paige..." His voice was taut with suppressed emotion.

She moved toward him as if in a trance.

"Paige...for God's sake..."

She came to stand directly in front of him and splayed her hands across the rippling muscles of his chest. She heard him groan as the liquid softness of his gaze encouraged her lips to reach up and gently come to rest against his. In that moment, they were both lost.

Their love making was fierce, almost savage in its intensity. There wasn't a portion of Paige's body left untouched by Lane's hands or lips. She was with him, and they melted together as one.

The dawn saw them still entangled in each other's arms. Paige was the first to awaken. An uneasy feeling in the pit of her stomach made her break out in a cold sweat. She was sick.

Disengaging herself quickly from Lane's arms, she planted her unsteady feet on the carpet and practically ran to the bathroom. She was on her knees when Lane came stumbling in behind her. When he saw what was happening, he leaned over and held her head until her nausea was spent. Helping her up, he hastily wet a cloth and wiped her face and neck.

His face was grim as he silently helped her back into the bedroom and to the side of the bed. Tears pricked her eyes as she took in his still hostile expression.

It wasn't long, however, before she found out what caused his abrupt withdrawal.

"Are you pregnant again, Paige?" he demanded, his jaws clamped together.

His question rendered her speechless. When she finally found her voice, she stammered, "No...no." She shook her head, hoping to dispel the panic gnawing at her insides. "No...at least, I don't think..."

Lane interrupted harshly. "Well, if you are, you damn sure won't destroy this one!"

Astonishment, confusion and a deep hurt, hit Paige all at once. She reeled from the blow his words had dealt her.

He continued in a deadly calm voice, completely ignoring her outcry, *"I know about the baby you lost."*

Paige clutched her stomach to ward off the oncoming nausea.

Lane, taking advantage of her silence, continued. "You just couldn't wait to get rid of the baby, could you? Was having something that was a part of me so repulsive to you that you could actually destroy it on purpose?"

Paige's gasp stopped his flow of bitter words for a

moment. With eyes flashing, she cried, "Is that what you think I did—got rid of it?"

"Well, didn't you?"

Paige stared at him in horrified disbelief before turning her back and shutting him out completely. Words failed her once again. The tears were clogged in her throat, threatening to choke her.

The pain in her chest was so sharp it almost overwhelmed her. How could he even think she was capable of doing such a thing? And how had he found out about the baby? If he had known about the baby, why hadn't he come to her?

After what seemed like an eternity, Paige turned toward Lane and said without emotion, "If you don't know me better than that, then we're wasting our time discussing this or anything else for that matter." She paused, as she ran a hand tiredly over her eyes. "Please, just go away and leave me alone." Her voice was barely audible.

Lane's face was full of bitterness. "Don't worry. I'm leaving town, but I'll be back," he warned, his eyes on her face. "Then we'll talk."

Paige made her way toward the door. Setting her chin firmly, she told him in a tired voice, "You can't dictate to me any longer. I owe you nothing. My debt is paid in full."

An instant later, the door slammed behind her.

Paige remained in her room until she heard Lane's car back out of the garage. She watched from her bedroom window with tears rolling down her face. Then she let go and the tears turned to unrestrained sobs as time became meaningless. How long the sobs racked her body she didn't know. When they finally subsided, she felt utter desolation settle over her, smothering in its intensity.

Of one thing she was certain, she had no alternative but to leave Lane. He made it plain how he felt about her when he had accused her of deliberately losing their baby. Never would she let him know that, despite everything, she still loved him.

Tomorrow would be soon enough to pack and leave. At present, she was too exhausted to contemplate anything other than going to bed. After taking a nausea pill, which she kept on hand for her chronic queasiness, she pulled back the bedspread and crawled in between the sheets. However, sleep didn't come as readily as she had hoped. Emotionally drained, her thoughts centered around the possibility of another pregnancy. But the more she thought about it, the more convinced she became that she was definitely not pregnant.

She had had none of the symptoms of last time, including the nausea. Anyway, two years ago the doctor had told her that, due to complications following her miscarriage, it would be difficult for her to get pregnant again. So she held to the firm conviction that her nausea resulted from a nervous stomach and nothing else.

She slept during the rest of the day. It was early evening before she awakened. As she left her room, she encountered a concerned Joseph. He offered to bring her a bowl of homemade vegetable soup for dinner with a glass of iced tea, which she forced herself to eat. Then she returned immediately to bed and slept throughout the night.

The next morning she woke up early with the same uneasy feeling in her stomach. Taking deep breaths didn't help to settle the queasiness. When she reached the bathroom, she lost the contents of her stomach once again.

Deciding she definitely needed to see her doctor, she showered and dressed, hoping he could see her that morning. At nine o'clock she ramg his office and his receptionist told her to come in, but that she would have to be worked-in between patients.

Two hours later, Paige fought back tears as she drove down the freeway toward The Woodlands. Her thoughts were in turmoil. *I just can't be pregnant!* she told herself.

Numb by the time she reached home, she merely nodded at Joseph in passing and mumbled incoherently. "I'll be in my room. Please..." She paused to swallow a sob. "I—I don't want to be disturbed."

Joseph peered at her closely. "Mrs. Morgan, are you all right?"

"I'm fine," she told him as she made her way down the hall.

She stumbled to her bed, fell immediately across it and stared at the ceiling. The fact that she carried a life nestled within her body shed a completely different light on her plans. She had once told herself she wouldn't settle for less than Lane's love. She shrank from the thought of spending the rest of her life with a man who didn't love her.

She had no alternative except to rear the baby without a father's love and protection. The instant the doctor had confirmed her pregnancy, all other choices had been taken from her. Freedom? Career? Independence? What were they in comparison to her feelings for Lane and their unborn child?

Pain pierced her heart like an arrow. She wanted this baby desperately, and she didn't want to have it alone. Already she loved it, and she wanted Lane to love it, too. Even if he didn't love her she could stay with him and try to make their marriage work for the sake of their child. It would need both of its parents. Freedom, career and independence weren't important without Lane. She would gladly sacrifice them all for him and their baby.

As she considered these choices, fear grabbed at her heart. It could all come to nothing. What if Lane decided not to return home? What if she never got the chance to tell him about the baby? What if...

The pain was almost unbearable when she thought of all the unsolved problems between them.

Three weeks later Paige sat in the cool shade of the patio, knitting a baby blanket. Her only companion was a glass of lemonade. She stretched her back languorously as she sipped the cool liquid.

Today was not one of her better days. Her mother had spent most of the day with her, and as a result she was tired. Katherine's constant chatter had left its mark on Paige. And, too, she had to keep up the pretense that everything was fine between Lane and her.

Ever since the trial had ended Katherine couldn't say enough about her husband. He seemed to be her champion now. Lane was mellowing, Katherine said. His old hostility was wearing thin. And Jamie hardly drew a breath without making Lane the sole authority for everything.

Paige didn't understand Lane's past bitterness toward Katherine any more than she understood why their marriage had never worked. But the hostility had been there. If Katherine said it was healing, perhaps when Lane came home other things would heal.

Paige sighed and closed her eyes, allowing the tears to trickle down her face. She clung to the hope that he would come home at all. This one hope had kept her sane during the last three weeks.

The only difference that marked each day was the increasing signs of her pregnancy. At three months now, she was beginning to show due to her slenderness. She spread her hands across her stomach, trying to draw strength from the tiny life developing within her.

For a moment she thought her mind was playing tricks on her. Then she heard it again.

"Paige...?"

She opened her tear-stained eyes to see the haggard image of her husband standing before her.

He fixed his eyes on her as if she were a mirage. He blinked. "I didn't think you would still be here," he rasped with shocked emotion.

Paige was so relieved at seeing him, she bit down on her lip to keep from crying out loud.

As the dusk of the evening closed around them, their eyes locked with an impact that jarred them both. She heard, in the distance, the chirping of crickets. From the corner of her eye she saw the flicker of fire-flies.

Finally Lane took a hesitant step toward her, his movements jerky. There was pain in his voice as he said, "We have to talk."

"Yes, I know," she whispered.

Lane released a sigh as he sat down beside her, careful not to touch her. Paige's heart pounded. She was positive he could hear it.

He took a deep breath. "There's so much I want to say. I don't really know where to begin..."

Paige longed to reach out to him, but she couldn't, not until she knew what lay next to his heart.

"First of all, I want to apologize for so many things."

Unconsciously, she leaned forward. "Lane...I—"

"Shhh. Let me finish. I have to tell you all of it. I can't live with myself any longer if I don't." He clenched his teeth. Apology, Paige realized, didn't come easy to a man like Lane.

"When I came home from Europe that fateful day two years ago," he went on, "and found you gone, I felt I had been kicked in the stomach. I missed you, but pride made me seek a legal separation."

"As time passed, however, I couldn't seem to put

the pieces of my life back together without you. *You* were the missing piece."

"Oh, Lane, I…"

He went on as if she hadn't spoken. "Finally I realized I couldn't handle life without you any longer. It no longer mattered if you had a full-time career. All that really mattered was for you to come back home where you belonged. I was convinced we could work out our problems." He paused to wipe the moisture off his upper lip. "So I came to get you and bring you home."

Her expression was incredulous! She laid a hand on his arm nearest her and dug her nails into it.

"What did you say?" Her whispered words of agony fell heavily into the now silent evening.

"I said," he repeated humbly, "that I came to see you at your mother's house."

"But…but," sputtered Paige, "where was I? I don't understand."

"It was the day after you…you lost the baby."

"Go on," she urged, swallowing.

"Katherine answered the door. Obviously out of her concern for you, she tore into me, hurling all types of accusations in my face." He paused, holding her wide-eyed gaze. "She all but told me in so many words that you no longer wanted me, nor my baby." He swallowed hard as his voice thickened. "She told me that you had aborted…" The words stuck in his throat and he couldn't go on.

"No!" Paige screamed like a wounded animal as

she leapt up from the lounge chair before Lane could stop her.

She ran dry-eyed to her room and threw herself across the bed. The pain was so intense it froze the tears within her. No wonder Lane had shown bitterness toward her and Katherine. No wonder he felt the injured party. He had every reason to feel as he did.

She began to cry. The sobs racked her body with soul-wrenching depth.

She felt the mattress sink. ''Paige...please...I'm so sorry...'' Lane's voice was torn. ''Don't cry anymore. I can't stand it.''

He never touched her as he continued to free his soul of long-endured pain. ''When Katherine said *that* word, I went crazy. I turned and jumped into the car and drove off like a deranged person. For two years, I've lived with poison running through my veins. You see, I wanted that baby. I—'' His voice broke.

She whirled around to stare at him in disbelief. ''But, Lane, you must have known I could never—''

''I know,'' he interrupted bitterly, ''but your mother was so convincing...'' He drew an unsteady breath. ''I knew deep down that she had lied but never could bring myself to admit it until...''

''Until...'' she prodded, her throat suddenly constricted.

''Until you came to my office that day. My first thoughts upon seeing you were to punish you for what I thought you had done to me, to my child.'' He paused, holding her gaze. ''But after you ran out on me again, I panicked for the third time in my life. It hit me that I had been fooling myself. In order to continue to survive, I knew I must have you.''

''But, I don't...'' she began, only to be cut off in midsentence.

''I knew I had to find a reason to force you back into my life. So when I heard your story about Jamie, I felt I had indeed been given a second chance.''

Hope surged through her. She waited with bated breath.

He rubbed a hand over his eyes before he continued. ''I would've helped Jamie regardless. And Wallace, he, too, was just another ploy to get you back into my arms.''

''Oh, Lane,'' she whispered brokenly, ''we've wasted so much time.''

''I know,'' he breathed achingly. ''Can you ever forgive me?''

She shook her head, trying to clear it. ''I nearly died when I lost our baby. I truly didn't want to live because not only had I lost the baby, but you as well. For a while I hated you with a passion. I needed you so much and you let me down. So after I recovered, my work became the most important thing in my life.'' She paused. ''Until I saw you again.''

She heard the sharp intake of his breath as he moved closer. ''Then can you really find it in your heart to forgive me for my blind stupidity?'' He paused, searching her face. ''And for all the things I've said and done to hurt you since we've been back together—especially Jill and the money clip? She lied...''

"Don't..." Paige interrupted, placing a finger against his lips. "That's no longer of any importance. All is forgiven," she finished tremulously.

With those words, Lane held her eyes with a tenderness that seemed to draw the very soul from her. The full moon cast a warm glow over the room. In the hush of the night, time became an intruder.

The grooves around his mouth deepened to suggest a smile as he reached for her. A wild longing surged through her as she went into his arms.

Time had passed for words. Even the secret that lay nestled within her would have to wait. This moment in time was theirs to come together in love.

Paige ached with an unfulfilled need as Lane's mouth sought the fullness of hers. He kissed her hungrily, folding her closer until their hearts thundered as one.

With a groan he tore his mouth away from hers and said, his breath warm, "I love you! I love you!"

Her insides quivered at his declaration. She was on fire for him. She pulled his knit shirt out of his jeans and ran her hand up his back, kneading his muscles, and then around to his chest where she pulled and tugged on his tiny buds.

Paige heard him groan as he quickly pulled himself away from her, reaching over and untying the straps of her halter top. Wasting no time, he lowered it, feasting his eyes on the burgeoning fullness of her breasts. They beckoned his touch as the moonlight drew patterns across their roundness. Lane felt them with his hands and then his mouth. Paige crumbled at the sensuous assault on her body. She cried out in delight as he laid her head against the pillow and gently removed her dress.

He then stood up and quickly shed his clothing. Upon returning to the bed, Paige grabbed his head and said in a whisper, "I love you, Lane Morgan, more than life itself."

In the moonlight, his eyes shone. "And I you, Mrs. Lane Morgan."

She lowered his head down to hers and drew strength from his lips. When the kiss ended, he bent over her and gently painted a circle of love with his tongue on her rounded stomach. Pure lust rippled throughout her being at his intimate touch.

For a moment, however, his wandering tongue ceased. Her heart skipped an exciting beat. She waited for him to say something, but the moment passed as he continued his labor of love bringing her to untold heights of rapture.

They paid loving homage to each other's bodies throughout the night until the dawn saw them spent in each other's arms.

Lane was the first to awaken. He nuzzled Paige's ear with his tongue. "Wake up, sleepyhead," he purred.

She smiled contentedly as she stretched every bone in her body. She winced as he slightly grazed a tender breast.

Lane's eyes darkened at her show of pain. "Did I hurt you, my darling?" he questioned huskily.

"No." Her smile deepened. "At least, not much."

He groaned. "I can see now there'll be no morning romp." He grinned impishly.

She turned to him in amazement. "You mean you want more?"

"If I live to be a hundred, I'll still want more of you." His eyes grew serious. "Does that answer your question?"

She flashed him a beautiful smile.

His hands were very tender, very sure as he touched her body. Her breasts more than filled his large hand as he brought them to life once again. He then moved with his hands to caress her stomach.

Before Paige realized his intention, he threw back the sheet and fastened his eyes on her body. He began at her toes and moved his eyes slowly upward.

A strangled sound came from his throat as his gaze rested on the bulge in her lower stomach and then moved upward to her full breasts. After a timeless moment, he asked, "Are you carrying my child?" His voice was filled with awe.

"Yes," she told him softly.

His answer was to lean over and gently kiss the place where the object of their love lay nestled. Paige felt his tears as they branded her where they fell. It was an emotional moment, one in which Paige felt her heart turn over.

When he lifted tear-edged eyelashes toward her, she reached out and wrapped her arms around him. "I can't believe I've been given another chance," he whispered, searching her face with joyous intensity. "And this time I'm not about to make any mistakes.

I want you to have everything—your own jewelry store—in fact, I insist on it.'' He paused thoughtfully, ''Believe me, my darling, I've learned how to share.''

Paige's eyes were tender. ''Right now,'' she said softly, ''the only thing I'm interested in is you and the baby. Maybe later, I'll think about going back to work. About Mother. About Jamie. About everything that's happened.''

Lane's eyes darkened as he cupped her chin in his hand. ''Babies have a way of bringing mothers and daughters together like they do husbands and wives. You'll see.''

Paige began kneading the smooth skin of his shoulders. ''I know,'' she sighed heavily, ''I won't pretend it will be easy, but in time...''

Lane pressed her closer to him. ''The healing process takes a while, my love, but we have all the time in the world—all the time in the world,'' he repeated huskily.

New York Times **bestselling author**

BARBARA DELINSKY

Stranded on an island off the coast of Maine...

Deirdre Joyce and Neil Hersey got the solitude each so desperately craved—but they also got each other, something they hadn't expected. Nor had they expected to be consumed by a desire so powerful that the idea of living alone again was unimaginable.

But was blazing passion enough to keep them together? Or could this be...

THE REAL THING

Available in February 1998 where books are sold.

The Brightest Stars in Women's Fiction.™

MIRA

Look us up on-line at: http://www.romance.net

MBD438

Coming in March 1998
from *New York Times* bestselling author

Jennifer Blake

**The truth means everything to Kane Benedict.
Telling it could destroy Regina Dalton's son.**

Down in Louisiana, family comes first—that's the rule
the Benedicts live by. So when a beautiful redhead starts
paying a little bit too much attention to his grandfather,
Kane decides to find out what the woman really wants.

But Regina's not about to tell Kane the truth—that she's
being blackmailed and the extortionist wants Kane's
grandfather's business…or that the life of her son is
now at stake.

Available where books are sold.

**The Brightest Stars
in Women's Fiction.™**

Look us up on-line at: http://www.romance.net

Detective Jackie Kaminsky is back—and this time *First Impressions* aren't adding up…

Second Thoughts

Jackie Kaminsky had seen enough break and enters to know that intruders usually took something. This one left a calling card and a threat to return. The next visit was from a killer. Jackie had a list of suspects, but as they became victims, too, she found herself thinking twice about *everything* she thought she knew—professionally and personally.…

"Detective Jackie Kaminsky leads a cast of finely drawn characters."
—*Publishers Weekly*

MARGOT DALTON

Available in March 1998 wherever books are sold.

The Brightest Stars in Fiction.™

From national
bestselling author

SHARON
SALA

SWEET BABY

So many secrets...

It happened so long ago that Tory Lancaster can't
recall being the little girl who came home to an
empty house.

A woman now, Tory is trying to leave behind the
scarring emotions of abandonment and sorrow—
desperate to love, but forever afraid to trust. With the
help of a man who claims to love her, Tory is able to
meet the past head-on—a past haunted by images of
a mysterious tattooed man and the doll that was her
only friend. But there are so many secrets, so
little time....

Available in February 1998
at your favorite retail outlet.

**The Brightest Stars
in Women's Fiction.™**